LINGERING SHADOWS

A CHRISTIAN ROMANCE BOOK 1 IN THE SHADOWS SERIES

JULIETTE DUNCAN

COPYRIGHT

PRAISE FOR "LINGERING SHADOWS"

"Lingering Shadows is well written and the story pulled me in, and I have high hopes for the rest of the series. Readers are left with a cliff hanger of an ending but given the plot, it made total sense. Kudos to the author for not shying away from some touch topics." *Love Reading*

"Excellent. Riveting and so real. I appreciated the depth of this story. I'm onto #2!" *Ashley*

"Am a very big fan of Christian novel, Lingering Shadows reminds me of myself in some ways and how God's unfailing love never gives up on us. I can't wait to read more inspiring books from Juliette Duncan." *Florence*

"Very refreshing to read a story that followed real life and a story that relates to an issue concerning a problem many people have and face on daily routine also a Romantic novel without all the sex and the language that goes with it." *Jean*

CHAPTER 1

*N*orth East England 1981

MARRYING DANIEL O'CONNOR WAS A RISK, no two ways about it. Lizzy still didn't know why she'd agreed to marry him, but tomorrow at midday, come what may, she would be saying "I do".

Although impetuous, she was also loyal, and while her actions were highly irregular, she *would* see it through, and she *would* be a good wife to Daniel, regardless of what anyone thought. And she'd prove her father wrong.

She would also ask God to bless their marriage, even though Daniel didn't yet share her beliefs.

THE PAST WEEK had been busy, keeping her mind off tomorrow, and now she had to collect Sal, her best and most loyalist of friends, from the station. Lizzy glanced at her watch and tapped her fingers on the steering wheel as the traffic stalled in front of her.

"Come on, you lot! I don't want to be late. Move!" She thumped the wheel, and then sped around the car in front that had completely stopped and was going nowhere.

The train pulled into the station just as she entered the car park. She zipped into a spot someone had just vacated, jumped out of the car, slammed the door, and sprinted to the entrance, taking the stairs two at a time. People of all sizes and shapes were already piling out of the train onto the platform, but Sal's carrot red hair stood out amongst the crowd, making her easy to spot.

"Sal!" Lizzy waved and called out, not worried in the slightest what the people around her would think. Running down the stairs against the general flow of traffic, she bumped into anyone who wasn't fast enough to get out of her way, and almost knocked Sal off her feet when, finally reaching her, she threw her arms around her best friend with uncontrolled abandon.

"I'm so glad you could make it, Sal. It's great to see you!" Lizzy whirled her around and hugged her again.

"Wow Liz! It's great to see you too, but it's only been three months!" Sal drew her eyebrows together and tilted her head slightly, curiosity loitering in her smile as she searched Lizzy's face. "Are you okay?"

Lizzy pulled back, annoyed at Sal's perception. "Of course I'm okay. What makes you think I'm not?"

"Oh, you just seem a little on edge."

Lizzy's eyes narrowed and her lips flattened into a thin line as she picked up Sal's dark brown carry all.

"I'm fine."

"Okay then." Sal glanced at Lizzy from the corner of her eye before tucking her arm through the crook of Lizzy's elbow as they walked back along the platform. "I still can't believe you moved all the way up here. Couldn't you have gone somewhere just a little closer?"

"You know why I did." Lizzy breathed in deeply. "Oh, but Sal, I do miss home." Lizzy fought back the sudden tears that pricked her eyes, and then turned her head to Sal, a forced smile planted on her face. "But enough of that. Tell me everything that's been happening."

All the way to the car, the girls chatted like two long lost friends, and Lizzy's mind was taken off the events of the morrow yet again.

THE TRAFFIC HADN'T LESSENED, and as she pulled out of the car park, Lizzy turned on the wipers. *A wet day. Great. That's all I need.*

She slammed on the brakes as a car pulled out in front of her, and blasted the horn while she shouted at the driver, a futile exercise, but it made her feel better. Her nerves were a little on edge.

"You haven't told your parents yet, have you?"

Lizzy bristled and held the steering wheel a little tighter. *Why did Sal have to bring my parents up?* She shook her head without looking at Sal.

"Don't you think you should?"

Lizzy clenched her jaw. *Why can't she let things be? Maybe asking her to come was a mistake.* But Sal was her best friend.

She put her foot down to beat the lights that had just changed to amber. "No. And I don't feel bad about it. They'd never agree to me marrying him, so I'm just going to do it. I know they'll be angry when they find out, but it'll be too late to do anything about it then. They shouldn't have been so horrible to him."

"Are you sure you know what you're doing, Liz? Have you prayed about it?"

Sal's eyes bored into her. Lizzy wasn't game to look. *Maybe I should tell her how I'm really feeling.* But if she knew the truth, Lizzy was sure that Sal would try her best to stop her from marrying Daniel, and it wasn't worth the risk. Having set her path, Lizzy was determined to stick to it. She'd actually contemplated calling it off a few times over the past couple of weeks, but the prospect of being alone again made her banish those thoughts immediately. It had to be better to be with someone than to be lonely.

Lizzy took a deep breath and calmed herself. "Yes, I've prayed about it. And yes, I do love him. I know what I'm doing, Sal, even if you think I don't." She slowed down to take the next corner. "He's a bit of a lad, so different to Mathew, but I love him. He makes me laugh and smile. I feel happy when I'm with him." She turned her head and glanced at Sal. "I know what you're thinking, and you might be right. I probably am marrying him on the rebound, but you know what? I don't care. I can't handle being on my own any longer." She wiped the tears from her eyes and hoped Sal hadn't seen them.

Sal looked at her intently. "I hope you'll be happy, Liz. I really do."

THEY SAT QUIETLY the rest of the way to Lizzy's apartment on the outskirts of town. The street lights had come on early, and the drizzle had increased to light rain. The windscreen wipers were doing their thing, and their squeak reminded Lizzy she needed to get new blades.

"This is it. Home sweet home." Lizzy pointed to the block of apartments on the left as she reversed into a small gap on the narrow street lined with cars. Four storeys high, and spanning half a block, the complex's only redeeming feature was the garden that ran between the brown brick walls and the footpath. "It's better on the inside," she said as she saw the look on Sal's face.

"I would hope so!" Sal raised her eyebrows. "A bit of a come down, Liz. "Are you going to live here once you're married?"

"For a while. It really is much better on the inside." Lizzy opened the car door and climbed out. She zipped her jacket and covered her head with its hood before grabbing Sal's bags out of the boot and directing her up the flight of stairs. Opening the door to the apartment, she held her breath as she waited for Sal's reaction.

"Wow, Liz! You weren't wrong! This really is nice!" Sal entered the living room and fell onto the new sofa Lizzy had picked up recently at a sale. "You always did have an eye for nice things."

"Thanks Sal." Lizzy's face expanded into a broad grin. "I'll just put these in your room and then make us a drink."

Lizzy placed Sal's bags in the spare room, and then busied herself making a cup of tea. She glanced at the clock. Daniel would be here any minute.

∼

"Liz! I know you told me he was good looking, but you didn't tell me how much!"

"Shh! He'll hear you!"

"Okay, I'll just sit here and drool."

"He is pretty cute, I have to agree." Lizzy laughed and glanced over to where Daniel was standing at the bar, and her heart warmed. Maybe she did love him after all.

"Here you go, my lovelies! Two shandies with flair!" Daniel placed the glasses on the table and winked at Sal.

"Daniel! You shouldn't do that! What will she think!" Lizzy said with a laugh in her voice.

"Oh, go on," he said in his best Irish accent. "I was just having a bit o' fun!"

"It's okay, Liz." Sal patted Lizzy's leg and then looked up, a warm smile on her face. "Thank you, kind sir."

"My pleasure." He bowed, and then took his seat beside Lizzy. He placed his arm around her shoulders, and pulled her close. She didn't resist, instead, she snuggled closer.

"Good of you to come up for the wedding, Sal," Daniel said. "Lizzy's told me a lot about you."

"Has she just?" Sal glanced at Lizzy with a glint of mischief in her eye. "And what exactly has she been saying?"

"Oh, only good things," Daniel replied.

"I'm pleased to hear that!" Sal said.

"And what has she told you about me?" Daniel raised his eyebrows.

Sal hesitated and stole a glance at Lizzy before replying. "Only good things!"

Both girls burst out in laughter at Sal's attempt to copy his accent. Lizzy sat up and smiled at Daniel. As their eyes met, a tingle of excitement ran through her body. Cheeky he might be, but he was also lovable. And he was going to be her husband.

"Come on you two! You'll have enough time for that tomorrow!" Sal said.

Lizzy turned her head and grinned at Sal. "Yes, you're right. Let's order, shall we?"

As Lizzy laughed and reminisced with Sal over dinner, her heart lightened and her anxiety over her forthcoming wedding lessened. For a while at least.

When she climbed into bed a few hours later, however, her active mind kept her awake. Did she really know what she was doing?

CHAPTER 2

*L*izzy woke early from her restless sleep and peeked out the window. The sun was nowhere to be seen, just thick black cloud hovering in the sky, just like the cloud that hovered in her heart.

She propped her pillows behind her and sat up. She reached for her Bible, but could only stare at the cover. What if she read something she didn't want to hear? No, she couldn't risk that. Closing her eyes, Lizzy tried to pray, but instead, she drifted off to sleep.

She woke with a start when Sal placed a cup of tea on the dresser beside her bed some time later. Sal sat down and took her hand.

"Hey."

"Hey yourself." Lizzy looked at her friend and smiled warmly. The knot in her stomach she didn't know was there loosened. No need for words. They knew each other so well after all they'd been through. Her heart lifted knowing Sal was here to support her on this day. Lizzy wished she could talk honestly, but probably had no need. Sal knew.

"Come on, kiddo. We need to get you ready for your big day." Sal stood and opened the curtains. "I think that man of yours is champing at the bit to marry you."

Lizzy laughed at the thought. How many times had he suggested they run off and get married at Gretna Green? And how many times had she told him they were almost doing the same thing, anyway?

She straightened herself and sipped her tea. This was it. She would go ahead with the wedding, right or wrong. She lifted her head and her eyes met Sal's. "Okay, kiddo, let's get this show on the road."

THE HOUR or so she and Sal spent at the beauty salon having their hair and make-up done had been relaxing, but now they were back at the apartment, and the time had come to get ready.

"Do you want something to eat before we begin?" Sal called out as she put the kettle on. "I think I'll have a cup of tea and some toast."

"Mmm, maybe not." Lizzy rubbed her stomach. "I don't know I could eat anything."

Sal looked at her tenderly. "Are you sure you're okay?"

Lizzy paused for a moment and took a breath. "Yes, I'm fine. It's just hard to believe it's all happening." She smiled at Sal and reached for the cross hanging around her neck. "I'll go fetch my dress."

She'd chosen a simple dress to get married in. After all, it was a morning wedding at the Register Office. A full blown wedding gown would have been over the top.

"Come on, let me do that." Sal placed her tea and toast on the table and took over from Lizzy.

Maybe she could have done it herself, but Lizzy's hands were shaking, and she was having trouble doing up the little buttons on the front of the bodice. As she stood there while Sal battled with each tiny button, she was aware of the clock ticking. *Not much longer now...*

"There you go! Let me look at you." Sal stepped back and Lizzy turned around slowly. "Beautiful!"

"Thank you, Sal." Lizzy looked at herself in the mirror. Maybe she did look beautiful today. Well, almost. Beside Sal she often felt very plain, but today, with her hair done nicely and her make-up done properly, and wearing the dress the shop attendant had insisted suited her perfectly, maybe she did look beautiful.

THE TAXI ARRIVED and Lizzy and Sal walked carefully down the stairs and climbed into the back seat. The rain that had been threatening still held off, and although the sky was still grey, small patches of blue were visible in the distance. Maybe the sun would beat its way through the clouds and shine down on this day after all. She could always hope.

"Are you nervous?" Sal asked as the taxi made its way along the streets towards the town centre.

Lizzy looked down at her hands before replying. "A little."

"I'm not surprised. It's not too late, you know." Tears formed in Lizzy's eyes at Sal's gentle, caring tone. Sal reached out and squeezed Lizzy's hand. "You don't have to go through with it, you know."

Lizzy looked out the window, forcing her tears to stop. It wouldn't do to turn up at her wedding with red eyes and mascara blackening her cheeks. She pulled a tissue out of her purse and dabbed her eyes. With the flow of tears stopped, she took control of herself, and turned back and looked at Sal. "I'm okay. I know it's not what I wanted, but Daniel loves me, and I do love him. It's just last minute nerves, that's all."

"Okay then." Sal squeezed her hand again. "If ever you need to talk, you know where I am."

THE TAXI PULLED up outside the Guildhall. On a sunny day, the dark coloured sandstone building would have looked more appealing, but on this dreary winter's day, it looked cold and unwelcoming. A sudden gust of wind hit as they alighted from the cab. Lizzy shivered and pulled her coat tighter.

"This is a beautiful old building, Liz," Sal said as they entered the foyer. Looking around at the plush furnishings and artwork, Lizzy had to agree it was indeed a much nicer building inside than out.

Sal's gaze settled on Lizzy. She stepped closer and tucked a piece of hair that had been blown in the wind back into place. "Are you sure you're okay, Liz? Last chance."

Lizzy stood steadily and reached for Sal's hand. "Yes, I'm sure. Let's go find everyone."

They found the small room that had been allocated for the ceremony without any problem. Before they entered, Lizzy stopped and inhaled deeply. For a moment, she wanted a crystal ball. Was she doing the right thing? Was she really ready for this? Neither she nor anyone else had one, so she held her head high and entered the room with Sal beside her.

THE FIRST PERSON she saw was Daniel. Always the life of the party, today he was no different. The fears of her heart melted away when he winked at her. She looked into those cheeky blue eyes and saw the man who had swept her off her feet only months before.

She'd first laid eyes on him at his cousin Nessa's thirtieth birthday party. A fine autumn evening, Lizzy had been looking forward to getting out after being house bound with all her school work. Nessa had befriended her at church, and was keen for her to make some friends. This was the perfect opportunity, she'd said.

The party began with cocktails in Nessa's garden. Lizzy wore a long Indian type skirt and felt almost bohemian. She stood with Nessa, chatting to a couple of girls she'd just been introduced to, when Nessa called a dark haired young man over to join the group.

"Everyone, this is my cousin Daniel from Belfast. Daniel, this is Susan, Lizzy and Brianna."

"Pleasure to meet you lovely ladies." He bowed with a flourish, and then asked if he could get the girls a drink.

"Thanks, but I'm okay at the moment," Brianna replied. Lizzy just shook her head and laughed. She'd never heard such an intriguing accent before. She thought it suited him. He was far too attractive to just sound normal.

"How long have you been here?" Susan asked.

"Oh, going on two weeks now. Bonny place."

"You really think so?" Brianna asked. "I've always thought it was rather a boring backwater type town, myself."

"I guess it's what you compare it with. I think it's grand. There's the river, and the sea not far away, and the pubs. A lot of pubs." He cocked one eyebrow and grinned. "Are you girls from here?" He looked at each of the girls in turn, but his cheeky eyes caught Lizzy's and she was mesmerized by them for a fleeting second.

She let out a huge breath when Susan answered first, because it took her a moment or two to gather herself. Susan and Brianna had both replied, so now it was her turn. She didn't want to tell him she was from the south, but Lizzy figured he'd know as soon as she opened her mouth.

"Oh, we've got a posh one here." His eyes sparkled and then he winked at her.

"I'm not really." Lizzy lifted her chin to a haughty angle and glared at him. "My family might be, but I'm not. I'm just an ordinary person, doing an ordinary job."

"Posh **and** fiery! And what job might that be?"

"I'm a teacher." She looked him straight in the eye.

"That's a grand job. Teachers are the backbone of our society, don't you agree?" Susan and Brianna both nodded. They appeared to be fascinated by this gregarious, cheeky man, but it was Lizzy he was interested in, so it turned out. He took her arm when dinner was announced, and led her to a table where they dined together and engaged in friendly banter for the next hour or so.

When the music started, he led her to the floor, and literally swept her off her feet.

"You dance very well, Elizabeth," he whispered in her ear, causing her pulse to race. Being from a 'posh' family, she certainly knew how to dance, but she'd never danced like this before. What would Mother think if she could see her now? Casting that thought aside, Lizzy decided to enjoy the moment. Perhaps he was holding her just a little too close, but she didn't push him away.

Lizzy didn't know what he saw in her. She was plain, nowhere near as attractive as either Susan or Brianna, but he was taken with her, and she with him. Maybe her rebellious spirit had attracted him. Whatever it was, they spent the rest of the evening together, and when it came time to leave, he asked if he could see her again. She didn't hesitate. She was ready for this. *Maybe at last I can forget Mathew.*

"Lizzy! There you are! And what a treat for sore eyes, might I say!" Daniel strode towards her and was about to wrap his arms around her when his mate, Johnno, stepped between them.

"Uh, uh - none of that yet. Wait until you've tied the knot, man."

"Get outta here, Johnno. Can't I give my lady a peck on the cheek?"

"Wait until you're legally wed. It's bad luck if you kiss her beforehand."

"Says who?"

"Says me."

"Okay then. Well, let's get this show on the road, and then I can kiss her all I want - right?" He looked at Johnno, and then at Lizzy. "Lizzy, you ready?"

"Yes Daniel, let's do this." She smiled at him. How handsome he looked in his pin striped suit. He loved wearing nice clothes, but the suit made him look suave and sophisticated. A thrill of excitement ran through Lizzy's body at the thought of being alone with this man later in the day.

Only ten people were present, plus the officiating celebrant. Daniel, Lizzy, Sal, Daniel's cousin Nessa and her husband Riley, Daniel's mate John, Lizzy's fellow teachers, Janine and Robert, and her friends from church, Colin and Linda. Colin had agreed to give her away.

"Colin, let's go." She hooked her arm in his as Daniel and Johnno took their places beside the celebrant. Sal led the way, and stood to the side when she reached the front. Lizzy walked the whole ten metres with her eyes glued on Daniel's. Colin's hand on hers helped to steady her pounding heart, and she tried not to think of anything apart from marrying Daniel, but in those fleeting moments, images of Mathew and her parents flitted through her mind. *Oh God, not now. I can't deal with it. Later. I promise. Later.*

Colin placed her arm in Daniel's when they reached the front, and gave her a reassuring squeeze before taking his place beside Linda. She heard very little of the ceremony. Like an out of body experience, happening to someone else. Not to Elizabeth Walton-Smythe of Wiveliscombe Manor in Taunton Deane.

The familiar words pulled her out of her trance, and back to the here and now. She'd heard the words many times before at the endless weddings of distant relatives she'd been forced to attend, but now it was her turn.

"Do you, Elizabeth Anne Walton-Smythe, take Daniel Rorey O'Connor to be your lawful husband, to have and to hold from this day forward, for better, for worse, for richer, for poorer, in sickness and health, until death do you part?"

She looked at Daniel and saw the sparkle in his eyes. She took a deep breath.

"I do."

DANIEL GOT his way at last, and kissed her long and hard in front of everyone. She felt her cheeks flush, and pushed him away gently. He stole one more brief kiss before he turned her around and pumped his arm in the air.

Someone wolf whistled. She thought it was Johnno, and then everyone clapped. She saw the smiles on Sal's and Nessa's faces. It was real. It had really happened. She was now Mrs Elizabeth O'Connor.

THE WEDDING BREAKFAST was a noisy occasion. Daniel was in his element, and Lizzy could tell he was happy. He kept hugging and kissing her, and whispering words in her ear that made her blush. She knew it wouldn't be long before he'd want to leave, but to be honest, she wasn't in that much of a hurry now the time had come.

Sal sat on the other side of her, looking stunning in her green suit. Lizzy reached out and squeezed her hand.

"I wish you could stay longer, Sal." Lizzy's eyes teared up a little, and she quickly wiped them away, hoping Sal hadn't noticed.

"Oh sweetie, we'll catch up again soon enough." Sal returned her squeeze and smiled tenderly, almost causing Lizzy's tears to break free.

"I wish I could have come up earlier. Such a bother, this work business!" Sal's laugh lightened the moment, and Lizzy breathed easier.

"I agree. At least we've got a week off now. We'll have to catch up again soon, Sal. I don't know I can bear not seeing you."

"Come on, Liz. You've got Daniel to keep you company now." Lizzy caught Sal's eyes, and in that instant, what she'd done hit her like a ton of bricks. She was now married, for better or for worse, to Daniel O'Connor.

CHAPTER 3

*D*aniel and Lizzy left soon after. Daniel had planned their honeymoon, and all he'd told her was not to bring much. That wasn't very helpful, so she'd packed for almost all possibilities, just in case. As it turned out, she really didn't need much at all, as they stayed in their hotel room most of the following week.

He was a skillful lover, tender and kind, and their first week together was bliss. Lizzy had never imagined that married life could be so wonderful. Her mother had never spoken to her about what happened behind closed doors. The limited information she had as they began their marriage had been gleaned from the odd magazine and hushed whispers amongst her circle of friends at University. Never in her wildest dreams had she thought she could be so close to another human being.

They ventured out once or twice to get some fresh air, but

the chill wind of the north east coast soon drove them back inside into the warmth of each other's arms.

The week passed all too quickly, and before long they headed back into town to start their real life together.

Not once had she thought of Mathew.

"COME ON DANIEL, I'm going to be late!" Lizzy grabbed her coat off the hook and opened the door. "I'll go without you," she called out playfully.

"Coming! Just give me a minute."

She looked back inside and saw him tying his shoe laces. His hair was rumpled and his shirt still undone, and as he stood, the sight of his bare chest made her insides quiver. She almost forgot she was in a hurry.

"I'm sorry, Lizzy. I'll be right there." He raced into the bathroom and she soon heard water splashing, and thought with dread about the mess he was making. Living with a man was certainly different to sharing a flat with a girlfriend, but it did have its benefits. Her mind started to replay their lovemaking of the previous night whilst she stood at the door waiting for him. Daniel had completely won her over with his constant tenderness and eagerness to love her at any hour of the day or night. It was no wonder he slept in.

"Well come on then, what are you waiting for?" He snatched a quick kiss as he flew past her.

Lizzy locked the door and ran down the steps, catching him as he reached the car.

She threw him the keys.

"You'd better drive today. I might be a bit late finishing this afternoon."

They climbed into the car, and took off towards Hull Elementary. She looked at her watch. They might just make it. The traffic seemed to be getting worse every day, but maybe it was because they were late every day. She'd never been late to school when she was single, but now, most mornings the bell was ringing as she jumped out of the car and sprinted to her classroom in an effort to beat the children.

Lizzy's preparation was suffering. How long would it be before she was spoken to about it? She muddled her way through each day, but she wasn't doing the best she could. Now Kids' Club was starting up again. Why had she agreed to it? Lizzy raced, yet again, into the classroom just ahead of the children.

"Good morning class." Lizzy stood with her hands on her hips, taking a number of slow, deep breaths, and surveyed the class of eight year olds standing before her.

"Good morning Mrs O'Connor." Her heart jumped as she once again heard the name. Still not used to it, every time Lizzy heard it, she thought of Daniel. A mental image of him pushing a trolley at the hospital flitted through her mind. It was the perfect job for him. He lit up anxious people's lives every day with his wit and humour, and he could whistle and sing as much as he wanted. The faintest of smiles played on her lips at the thought.

"Take a seat, class." She opened the folder on her desk and glanced inside. Normally she would have asked them to sit quietly, but this morning she let them talk amongst themselves for a few moments while she planned the day.

DANIEL ARRIVED BEFORE KIDS' Club had wrapped up. He leaned on the door frame of the activities room as she sat in front of the children, strumming her guitar whilst they sang a song she'd just taught them. His arms were folded, and the twinkle in his eyes suggested he was enjoying himself. The children gave her a strange look when she stumbled over some words and played the wrong chord. *Drat him for having this effect on me.* She tried to concentrate on the job at hand, all the while aware of him taunting her from the back of the room.

At the end of the song, the children turned around when they heard clapping. Lizzy shook her head as he came closer.

"That was lovely, children, and Mrs O'Connor."

She knocked the music stand over in her hurry to get up. "Children," Lizzy sighed and straightened her skirt. "this is Mr O'Connor. Say good afternoon."

"Good afternoon, Mr O'Connor," they all said in a sing song chant.

"And good afternoon to you, too," he replied in a similar fashion, making the children laugh.

"What are you doing?" she whispered sharply.

"Just thought I'd come and meet some of your little protegees. That's alright, isn't it?"

"Not really." She turned her back so the children couldn't hear. "Best if you wait outside in the car. We're finishing up now." She leaned closer. "I could get into trouble with you here."

"Okay, I'll go. Don't stress your pretty little head. Bye children. Nice to meet you." He waved as he walked back the way he came.

"Nice to meet you, too," they all called out.

"Miss, he sounds funny," a little blond haired girl said after he'd gone. They all laughed again.

"He's Irish, that's why," Lizzy said, quickly tidying up and dismissing the children.

THE PARENTS WERE all waiting outside, and once the children were handed over safely, Lizzy headed for the car. She'd calmed down a little by the time she reached it, but she still gave Daniel a good talking to.

"You just can't do that. You can't walk into a classroom full of children and take over." She folded her arms and glared at him.

"There there, Lizzy. I'm sorry. I just couldn't help it. I heard your sweet voice and the guitar music and it drew me in. I won't do it again, I promise." The twinkle in his eyes got her again. How did he manage it? Every time they had a disagreement, he'd sweet talk her and apologise; she'd forgive him, and then she'd end up in his arms.

It was hard to be angry with Daniel O'Connor for long.

THE FOLLOWING DAY, two things happened that rocked their almost perfect world.

CHAPTER 4

*L*izzy had just stepped into the shower when she heard the phone ring.

"Daniel, can you get that?"

"Sure, sweetie."

When he appeared in front of her several moments later with a startled look on his face, she wondered what had happened.

"You'd better get out. It's your mother."

Lizzy's mouth fell open and her body stiffened. They stared at each other for a moment. How could she have been so stupid? Her mother often called on a Friday morning.

"What am I going to say?"

He shrugged and shook his head. For once he had no words.

"You're a great help." She walked past him and picked up the receiver, taking a deep breath before speaking.

"Mother, how are you?"

"I'm fine thanks. How are you, Elizabeth?"

"Fine."

Her mother wasted no time.

"What's he doing there this time of the morning? I'm surprised at you, Elizabeth. We brought you up better than that."

"It's not what you think, mother."

"I thought we'd made it clear he was no good for you. Your father and I hoped we'd seen the last of him."

"No Mother. We're still together."

"I have to say I'm disappointed, Elizabeth." What was new? She always seemed to disappoint her parents.

"I'm sorry to let you down, Mother."

"Very well then. I was calling to say that your father and I would like to see you next Saturday on our way to Edinburgh. Maybe we could have luncheon together."

Lizzy paused before she answered, her mind racing as she digested this request. "It would be nice to see you, Mother. But Daniel will need to come. I hope you'll be okay with that."

"No, Elizabeth. Please don't bring him. You know what your father would be like. We'd much rather have luncheon just with you."

"Well, I'm sorry, Mother, but I won't come without him."

She heard her mother sigh on the other end of the line. Silence hung in the air between them. Lizzy pressed her hand hard against her chest and felt for her cross.

"If that's the way it has to be, I guess we'll just have to tolerate him." Lizzy rolled her eyes and looked at Daniel.

"Thank you, Mother. Do you have anywhere in mind?"

"You choose. But make sure it's a reputable place, will you?"

"Yes, Mother. I'll find somewhere suitable."

And with that, she ended the call. Lizzy held the receiver in her hand for a moment before replacing it. It had to happen eventually, but she'd successfully avoided having to tell her parents the truth for three whole months. There was no escaping it any longer.

~

DANIEL STOOD and stared at her, his eyes wider than normal.

"What did she say?"

"Lunch next Saturday. They're going to stop in on their way up north."

"And what did she say about me?"

Lizzy hesitated. How could she repeat her mother's words to Daniel? Why did her parents always consider themselves to be above everyone else? What right did they have?

"She said it would be alright."

"That's a lie, Lizzy, I can tell. What did she say?"

Lizzy grimaced and took a deep breath. She'd have to tell him.

"She said they'll tolerate you being there."

"Tolerate! Who do they think they are? I've a good mind to give them some of their own back."

"Oh Daniel. Don't be like that." She reached out to him, but he pushed her away. "You know what they're like. We've just

27

got to be better than that and not let them get to us." She reached out again, but this time he backed away. "We're going to have to tell them. We can't put it off any longer."

He turned and thumped his hand against the wall.

"God help me, Elizabeth. I'm going to need patience."

Lizzy needed to sit down. She felt faint. The last time she'd seen Daniel like this was the day they'd stormed out of her parent's place at Christmastime. Her heart fell as she recalled that moment.

~

IT WASN'T as if he'd done anything wrong. Her mother and father, particularly her father, were snobs. How they professed to be Christians was beyond her.

They were an intimidating couple at the best of times. She thought Daniel had handled himself very well. but they'd obviously thought differently.

"He's just an uncouth Irishman, Elizabeth," her father had said as they stood in the morning room where she'd been summoned half an hour earlier. "I don't know why you're wasting your time with him." She held her hands together to stop them from shaking. His cold eyes were fixed on hers and he looked her up and down before continuing.

"For God's sake, Elizabeth, we've brought you up better than this. Find yourself a real man for once." Roger threw his hands up in despair. "First you gallivant around with a Theology Student and now you degrade yourself with this, this...." He turned and looked at her mother, who'd been standing there allowing him to continue with his tirade. Lizzy was disgusted.

"You deal with her, Gwyneth. I can't handle this ludicrous nonsense."

Lizzy glared at her mother and dared her to continue.

"It's not that we don't like him, Elizabeth. It's just that we think you can do much better for yourself. Don't we, dear?" Her mother's subservience to her father angered her so much.

Lizzy breathed deeply and tried to control herself. How dare they talk about Daniel like that. She shook her head in disgust and turned away.

"He's not welcome here, Elizabeth," her father said sternly. "Don't bring him back."

"Don't worry. I won't." She strode across the room and slammed the door behind her.

Despite her outward bravado, her hands shook and she burst into tears as she fled for the sanctity of the garden, which was where Daniel found her.

"What's wrong with you, sweet girl?" She'd turned her head so he couldn't see her face, but he sat beside her on the garden bench and made her look at him. More tears fell and he wrapped her in his arms. Lizzy sobbed into his chest, unable to speak. She didn't want to tell him about the confrontation she'd just had with her parents. They could be so horrible. What wasn't there to like about Daniel O'Connor? He was funny and outgoing. He was friendly and courteous. He might have drunk a little too much at dinner, but she put that down to nerves. Who wouldn't be nervous meeting Roger and Gwyneth Walton-Smythe?

Her sobbing eventually eased, and she lifted her head.

Daniel handed her a handkerchief and she dried her tears before facing him. She studied his dark curly hair and his crystal blue eyes. Why did her parents have to ruin everything? She reached out and gently caressed his face with the back of her hand.

"We've got to leave, Daniel."

"Why? What's happened?" The concern in Daniel's eyes warmed her heart.

She felt for the cross hanging around her neck.

"I've just had words with Mother and Father."

He tilted his head and narrowed his eyes.

"What about?"

She shook her head. How could she tell him?

"No, I don't want to repeat it, Daniel. Let's just go."

Lizzy gritted her teeth and dug her fingernails into the palms of her hands. Their eyes locked together for what seemed an eternity.

"Was it about me?" Daniel finally asked.

Lizzy lowered her eyes and nodded. Tears began to well up again, and one after the other rolled down her cheek.

"What did they say, Lizzy?"

She sniffed, and wiped her face before slowly lifting her head. She couldn't speak.

Daniel's eyes had darkened, and his brow was furrowed. Lizzy's heart thumped in her chest. What would his reaction be if she told him? She couldn't imagine him accepting it happily. Who would? Maybe she should just tell him. Get it out in the open. It said more about her parents than anything else, although it would still be hurtful.

"Lizzy?" Daniel tilted his head.

She breathed in deeply and swallowed. *Oh God, please help me.* "They said I'm not to bring you back here."

Daniel leaned back and placed his hands on his thighs. His face darkened and his whole body tensed. Lizzy waited for the explosion.

"The two faced hypocrites. Who do they think they are! I've been nothing but nice to them. If they didn't like me, they should have told me to my face, not via you. I've a good mind to have it out with them." He jumped up and pummelled his fist into his other hand. A vein in his forehead pulsed.

She pulled on his arm.

"No Daniel. Let's just go. It would only make it worse if you saw them." She paused, hoping he'd see sense and calm down. She could only imagine the scene that would erupt if he confronted them.

Her eyes pleaded with him. "Please Daniel. Please."

Daniel's breathing calmed a little, but she didn't like the steely look on his face.

She placed herself in front of him and grabbed both his hands. Her heart thumped as she looked into his eyes.

"Daniel, I won't be coming back either. Let's go."

Lizzy exhaled slowly as she felt the tension in his body fall away. He pulled her close and wrapped his arms around her. She rested her head against his chest. Did she really mean what she'd just said? Could she choose Daniel over her parents? At this moment, yes, she could. Daniel loved her. She felt safe wrapped in his arms. Her father had never hugged her or made her feel loved. To him, she was just someone to control, to manipulate. Not the precious daughter she longed to be. No, she'd choose Daniel any day.

They held hands as they re-entered the house to collect their belongings. If she'd seen either of her parents, Lizzy would have turned away from them, but they were nowhere to be seen.

Taking one last look at the home she'd grown up in as they drove back down the driveway, Lizzy turned to Daniel and smiled, willing her tears to disappear.

Just outside the gates of Wiveliscombe Manor, Daniel stopped the car and took her hands in his.

She looked at him with puzzled eyes. "What are we doing, Daniel?"

"Shh." He lifted his right hand and slid a finger along her chin and traced her face slowly, all the way to the corner of her eye. The touch of his finger made her weak.

"Lizzy, I love you. I feel very honoured you chose me over your parents. I hope you won't regret it."

Lizzy shook her head slowly, captivated by his mesmerizing eyes.

"From the moment I saw you at Nessa's party, I knew you were the one for me. I know your parents don't think I'm good enough for you, but Lizzy, I love you, and I want to marry you." He squeezed her hand gently as he took a deep breath. "Lizzy, will you marry me?"

Lizzy's mouth fell open and her hand flew to her chest.

"Oh Daniel. Do you really mean it? Are you really sure?" She could hardly speak.

"Sure as I could be about anything."

She gazed into his eyes. Was this really happening? Did she love him enough to marry him? Could she say yes, knowing her parents would have nothing more to do with them?

Knowing his relationship with God was doubtful? But he loved her, and he'd made her forget Mathew. If she said no, what would happen? Would he leave her? If he did, she'd be beyond despair. Her mind was made up.

"Yes Daniel. I'll marry you."

~

LIZZY PULLED her towel tighter and looked up at Daniel, her eyes pleading with him to calm down.

"It had to happen sometime, Daniel. We knew that. We couldn't hide it forever." Her gaze lowered to her wedding ring. What would they say?

Daniel pulled her up and wrapped her in his arms.

"I'm sorry, sweet girl," he whispered as he kissed her neck. "We'll get through this."

It was going to be a long week, but at least they had each other.

THE OTHER EVENT was much happier. Unbeknown to Daniel, Lizzy had booked a doctor's appointment for that afternoon. She'd told him she'd be a little late as she had a few errands to do, and that she'd make her own way home.

She had her suspicions. She'd been sick just about every morning for the past two weeks, although she'd tried to hide it from Daniel.

Lizzy poured herself a second glass of water while she waited in the doctor's surgery. She couldn't sit still for long. Why did doctors always run late? Finally it was her turn. Dr

Richardson poked her head in the door and looked around at the waiting patients.

"Elizabeth O'Connor?"

Lizzy nodded and stood, and followed the doctor into her consulting room. She took a seat, and clutched her hands together.

The doctor gazed at Lizzy over the top of her glasses. "Well, young lady, your test has come back positive. You're going to be a mother. Congratulations!"

Lizzy's hand flew to her chest. She couldn't believe it. She was expecting!

"I hope your husband will be pleased," the doctor said.

"Oh yes, I'm sure he will be. I'll go home and tell him straight away. How far am I?"

"Eight weeks. And everything looks fine, but you need to come back for a check-up in two weeks' time."

LIZZY WALKED on air as she left the surgery. Surely this news would make it easier with her parents. It couldn't have happened at a better time. She thanked God for this miracle on her way home, and apologized for neglecting Him of late.

She couldn't wait to tell Daniel the news. He'd be so excited. She stopped at Tesco on her way home and picked out a nice piece of meat to cook for dinner to celebrate. She pictured it in her mind. Some pretty flowers picked from the garden in front of the apartment block to brighten their table, and a candle or two lit to create a romantic atmosphere. Quiet music playing in the background. She'd hold his hand, look into his eyes, and tell him he was going to be a father. His eyes would twinkle, and he'd wrap her in his arms and kiss her passionately. *He doesn't need an excuse to do that.* She giggled as she walked to the bus stop.

The bus ride home was uncomfortable. Friday afternoon rush hour, and there was no spare seat. If only the people around her knew she was a mother-to-be maybe she would have been offered one, but it was early days, and it definitely wasn't obvious yet to anyone apart from herself. And she really didn't need a seat. She was young, fit and healthy, but the smell of body odour from the man in front of her made her feel nauseous. She didn't want to make a spectacle of herself, so she peered out the window as best she could to take her mind off it.

The day had certainly thrown up some surprises. Whilst she'd been almost certain the doctor would officially announce her pregnant, the news that her parents were visiting next Saturday was a shock. She'd played the scene over in her mind a hundred times or more already, but she still didn't know how she would tell them their daughter had run off and married the man they'd evicted from their home only months before, and that they were also going to be grandparents.

THE GARDENERS HAD BEEN BUSY, and the array of spring blooms adorning the footpath was enough to brighten anyone's day. Lizzy checked to make sure no-one was watching, and quickly picked a few brightly coloured geraniums and petunias before heading upstairs to the apartment. She hoped Daniel had stopped for a pint on the way home, as she wanted to have everything ready before he arrived. She wanted it to be perfect.

The apartment was quiet when she entered a few seconds later. It didn't take her long to unpack the groceries and put the meat in the oven. Walking into her bedroom to change out of her work clothes, she thought about what she should wear. Maybe the long Indian skirt she'd worn the night they met? Or perhaps the low cut summer shift she'd bought recently but hadn't worn yet. She decided on the shift. Maybe she'd even wear a little make-up. Yes, some blusher, mascara and lipstick. Not bad, Lizzy thought, as she stepped away from the mirror to get a better look. *Should I put my hair up?* She twisted it into a messy bun and secured it with a clip. *Yes, that's better.* She ran her fingers over her neck and down her chest, and closed her eyes, imagining they were Daniel's hands caressing her. She sighed in anticipation.

The smell of roast meat cooking suddenly hit her and brought her back to reality. She just made it to the toilet in time, and promptly brought up the whole contents of her day's food intake. She'd heard about morning sickness, but this wasn't morning. She never knew it would be like this.

Lizzy cleaned herself up, and headed back to the kitchen with a little less enthusiasm for cooking than before. Nevertheless, she still had important news to impart to Daniel, and so she set about preparing the vegetables and the table in readiness for his imminent arrival.

Everything was almost ready. She checked the clock. He should be home any minute. One last glance in the mirror. Yes, she still looked okay. A little pale maybe, but still more attractive than normal.

She put on her favourite music, the one they often made love to. She thought with a giggle that they might not even make it to the table. She glanced at the clock again and checked the meat and vegetables. Very nicely cooked. Maybe she should cut the meat and have it completely ready. It wasn't a job she liked, but she thought she could do it this time. Lizzy put her apron back on and carefully took the meat out of the oven and placed it onto the cutting tray. She attempted to control her breathing as another wave of nausea hit her. There was nothing left to bring up, or so she thought. Once again, she just made it, but this time she just heaved liquid into the toilet bowl. She almost cried. *When will Daniel be home?*

THE KEY in the door woke her, and she pulled herself up with a start. Lizzy didn't know what time it was, but she knew it was late. She'd turned the lights off hours before, and she must have fallen asleep in front of the television. She touched her eyes and knew they were puffy without even looking at them. Her hair had fallen out of its bun, and hung loose around her shoulders.

And then she remembered. Daniel hadn't come home for dinner.

She peered at him through the semi-darkness. He was trying to take his boots off. He was struggling, but she didn't get up to help. He was drunk. Tears rolled down her cheeks. Their perfect evening had been ruined.

He staggered towards the couch, and stopped suddenly when he caught sight of her.

"Lizzy." His whole body swayed. "You startled me, girl. What are you doing up?" He lurched forward and almost fell on top of her. She quickly moved out of the way before he landed on the couch beside her.

He was a mess. She recoiled from the smell of cigarette smoke and alcohol that oozed from his body. Lizzy had never seen him like this before. In fact, she'd never in her whole life been this close to an intoxicated person. She didn't like what she saw. This wasn't the Daniel she knew and had fallen in love with. She swallowed hard and fought back her tears.

"Where have you been, Daniel?" Lizzy narrowed her eyes and breathed heavily.

"Just havin' a few drinks wit the boys." He reached out for her arm, but she pulled away.

"I think you've had more than a few. And you can leave me alone, thank you very much."

"Oh Lizzy. I love you when you're angry." His eyes closed momentarily but then opened with a start. "I won ten quid."

"Well that's nice. On what, may I ask?"

"I beat the boys at pool. Ya shoulda seen me....." His eyes closed again.

She thought he'd fallen asleep, and she inched herself away from him. She'd almost made it, when he grabbed her and pulled her on top of him.

"Not so fast, Mrs O'Connor." His breath on her face made her queasy. "You haven't finished for the night. Come 'ere an give yur ole man some love." Lizzy recoiled as he fondled her breasts and tried to undress her. She resisted as much as she could, but he was strong. Stronger than normal. Maybe it was the drink. She succumbed and gave him what he wanted. But her heart and body were numb.

CHAPTER 5

*D*uring Lizzy's disturbed night, images of Mathew floated through her mind, and she didn't stop them. In fact, she relished them. Somehow they helped that horrid night to pass. Mathew would never have come home drunk. He didn't drink.

Lizzy allowed herself to relive the week she'd spent at his home in Portsmouth, almost three years ago.

HAVING COUNTED the days until she could see him again, Lizzy's heart burst with anticipation and excitement as the day finally came, and she drove the hundred or so miles from her family home in Taunton, where she'd spent most of the summer break, to Portsmouth, where his mother lived.

She tried to calm the butterflies in her stomach as she parked her car in front of his home, a semi-detached, less than ten paces wide, three streets from the harbour. For a few moments, Lizzy sat and studied the house, pulling herself together before she climbed out of the car and walked to the front gate. A whiff of fresh paint suggested that Mrs Carter, *Hilary,* had been doing some last minute preparations for her visit.

Taking a deep breath, Lizzy straightened her skirt and rang the bell. Her eyes lit up as Mathew opened the door. They gazed at each other for a moment, and then he smiled and hugged her. All the tension in Lizzy's body floated away as she hugged him back.

"So good to see you, Lizzy." His eyes sparkled and Lizzy's heart warmed. "Come on in. Mum's waiting to meet you."

He took her hand and she followed him into the tiniest kitchen she'd ever seen, well, apart from the one in her bed-sit accommodation at college, but that didn't count. And there she was. The mother she'd heard so much about. The mother who'd raised her two boys alone after their father had died in a traffic accident years ago. The mother who'd brought them up in the ways of the Lord and encouraged them both to go to Bible College to study for the ministry.

Hilary Carter greeted her with a warm kiss, and directed her to the table.

Lizzy relaxed and smiled at her. She took a seat beside Mathew, and reached for his hand, her heart beating faster as their hands joined. Hilary offered her tea and freshly cooked scones, and asked how her trip had been. Lizzy could see where Mathew's temperament had come from. A dainty, quiet, and particular lady, but also serious and perceptive. Lizzy felt scrutinized.

"How long have you lived here, Mrs Carter? It's a lovely home." Lizzy's heart fluttered as Mathew squeezed her hand.

"Since my wedding day. Thirty-three years next month," Mrs Carter replied wistfully, glancing at the photo taking pride of place on the wall directly opposite the kitchen. "Let me show you to your room, dear."

Lizzy followed her up the stairs, with Mathew trailing behind. The room was tiny, *and so close to Mathew's*. She sighed in frustration. It wouldn't be a problem. They rarely got any further than holding hands.

The week passed all too quickly. Every morning they ate their breakfast at the small round kitchen table. No radio. No television. No children. Occasionally she caught Mathew's eyes, and her heart exploded with love for him. Sometimes their legs touched under the table, but she was unaware of his mother noticing any of this.

They spent the week wandering around the harbour, discovering hidden coves and all sorts of remnants left over from the war. They read, talked, played games, and occasionally watched television.

But it was the memory of their last night together that brought tears to her eyes.

"Come on Lizzy, let's go for a walk." Mathew stood suddenly and grabbed her hand after dinner that night. She looked at him quizzically, and jumped up and followed him to the door. "Won't be long, Mum," he called out to Hilary in the back of the house.

"This is unexpected, but nice!" Lizzy snuggled closer as they strolled arm in arm along the street. The night air carried a slight chill, a wonderful excuse to cling to him.

They reached the park running along the water within minutes. The Gosport ferry's horn blasted into the night air not far away. Such a busy harbour. The old street lamps shed just enough light on the pathway, and cast strange shadows either side. Lizzy thought they'd head towards the main harbour area, but Mathew led her the other way along a path meandering through garden beds filled with perfumed roses and summer annuals. The heady smell assaulted her senses and made her think how nice it would be if he would only stop and kiss her. As she snuggled closer, his arm tightened around her and she breathed in his manly scent. Drawn by the mesmerizing sound of splashing water, they strolled towards the central fountain.

Taking a seat near the fountain, Mathew placed his arm around Lizzy and she rested her head on his shoulder.

"I know this week's been difficult for you, Lizzy." Mathew reached out and gently lifted her face. His lips were so close she could taste his sweet breath. Her heart pounded.

"I'm going to miss you, Elizabeth Smythe." His sparkling eyes looked deeply into hers as he traced her face with the tip of his finger. Her heart beat even faster as he lowered his head and brushed his lips against hers.

"Lizzy," he whispered as he held her face in his hands and kissed her gently.

If only this moment would last forever.

~

SUNLIGHT FILTERING through the flimsy curtains woke Lizzy the following morning. She opened her eyes just enough to see

Daniel sleeping beside her, and then curled her body into the fetal position and squeezed her eyes closed again.

Their honeymoon was over.

Tears rolled down her cheeks onto her pillow. *Drat you, Mathew. Why did you break it off?* Daniel grunted and rolled over. Lizzy turned her head and looked at him. If only it was Mathew lying there instead of Daniel. More tears trickled down her cheek. She wiped them away. But it wasn't Mathew she'd married. It was Daniel. A sudden wave of nausea hit her and she threw off the bed covers and raced for the bathroom. For a moment she'd forgotten she was pregnant.

WHEN LIZZY RETURNED to the bedroom, Daniel was leaning against the pillows. Considering the state he'd been in when he arrived home, she was surprised he didn't look worse. His hair was rumpled, and his eyes were bleary, but other than that, he didn't look much different to any other morning.

Lizzy stood in the doorway with arms folded, and glared at him.

"Well?" She broke the silence.

"I'm sorry Liz. I only meant to have a couple. I just got carried away." He tilted his head and reached his arms out. "Come and give me a cuddle."

Still upset, she wasn't prepared to forgive him that quickly.

"Was it the phone call that did it?" Lizzy's eyes narrowed.

He shrugged and breathed deeply, shaking his head.

"I don't know, Liz." He looked at her with puppy dog eyes. "Come here, sweet girl. I'm sorry."

Lizzy pursed her lips and sighed before climbing back into

bed with him. He wrapped her in his arms and kissed her neck. He lifted his face and looked her in the eye. "I really am sorry, Elizabeth. Will you forgive me?"

He looked sincere. Maybe she could forgive and forget this one time. She nodded and snuggled in close, but chastised herself for letting him off so lightly.

As THEY LAY SATISFIED in each other's arms a little later, Lizzy sat suddenly and wrapped the covers around her.

"Daniel, I need to tell you something."

"What is it, sweetie?" He sat up and looked at her with concern in his eyes. "Are you okay?"

Lizzy looked into his eyes and nodded, her face alight. "I've just been a little sick in the mornings. You might have noticed?"

He shook his head, but then his eyes widened.

"You're not...?"

She nodded her head and grinned, but she was unsure of his reaction.

"God be with us! I'm going to be a father! Come here you little beauty. Oh you precious thing." As she rested her head on his shoulder, tears welled in her eyes. *Perhaps if I'd told him last night, he wouldn't have been so rough...*

Lizzy watched in amazement as Daniel ran around and did everything. He made her rest while he cleaned the apartment. He made her cups of tea, and he even made dinner. Well, he didn't actually make it. He re-heated the dinner she'd cooked the previous evening. She lay on the couch reading a magazine, watching him out of the corner of her eye buzz around like an excited child. It was a strange but pleasant sight, and love for him smouldered and took root in her heart.

What a difference the news of their impending parenthood had made. At least for now, her parent's visit had faded into the background.

"I'll be able to teach him to ride a bike! I can take him fishing. I'll be able to play football with him. Oh, Lizzy, this is the best news yet!" It went on like that for the whole weekend.

THEN MONDAY CAME. Most days, Daniel dropped Lizzy at work and picked her up in the afternoon. She always had plenty to do in the classroom, and so was never too worried if he was a few minutes late. That Monday afternoon, she glanced at the clock and expected him to be there at any minute. She wanted to finish her planning for the next day, so she focused on what she was doing, trying to get it done before he arrived. The next time she looked at the clock, another hour had passed.

Lizzy stood and looked out the window. Neither Daniel nor the car were in sight. She packed up anyway. As she walked the short distance to the car park, she shivered and put on her jacket. Taking a seat on the brick retaining wall surrounding the car park, Lizzy checked her watch and looked out onto the road. All of a sudden her hands felt clammy. *What if he's had an accident?*

She stood and ran closer to the road. The cars were almost at a stand-still in the rush hour traffic. Lizzy peered both ways. He usually came from the left, but the white Ford Escort wasn't amongst the cars trundling along in either direction.

Maybe she should call the hospital? The phone box was just over the road. She took a deep breath to calm herself down. Just about to cross the road, her hand flew to her chest and she breathed a sigh of relief as the Escort came into sight.

"I'm sorry, sweetie, I lost track of time." Daniel reached over and opened the door for her.

Lizzy climbed in and looked at him. "You've been drinking." The relief she'd felt a moment earlier instantly disappeared.

He feigned a sad look and his cheeky eyes almost made her forget how annoyed she was. But it didn't work. Lizzy shook her head and narrowed her eyes. The memory of him coming home drunk just the other night was too fresh in her mind to allow her to forget that easily.

"The boys shouted me a few when they found out I was going to be a dad. That's all. Don't be angry, Lizzy love." He reached out and squeezed her leg.

"You'd better let me drive." She climbed out and strode around to the driver's side and opened the door. "Come on, Daniel... You're not driving like that. Get out."

"I do love you when you're angry, Lizzy." He planted a wet kiss on her cheek as he brushed past her.

She shook her head and climbed into the driver's seat. She was tempted to drive off without him. Her hands clenched the steering wheel as she entered the long line of traffic. She shot him a glance and gripped the wheel tighter. "I hope this isn't going to happen every day, Daniel."

He reached out his hand and placed it on her leg. "No Lizzy. It was just a one-off. I won't do it again." He squeezed her leg. She glanced at him again. The cheeky grin on his face made her think she was married to a naughty child.

CHAPTER 6

*O*nly it did happen every day. Lizzy grew angrier as Daniel returned later and later as the week progressed. The prospect of her parent's visit weighed heavily on her mind, and she guessed it weighed on Daniel's as well. Talking about it was impossible given his state of inebriation every night, and every morning they were in a hurry, and so it never happened.

Six pm Friday evening, she gave up waiting and called a taxi.

HOME ALONE, Lizzy heated a can of spaghetti for dinner. She didn't feel like anything at all, but she had to eat something for the sake of the baby. She took her plate and sat on the couch, put her feet up and flicked on the television. A tear rolled down her cheek as she stared at the screen.

How could she sit with her parents in the restaurant of the

Grand Hotel tomorrow lunchtime, and convince them she'd made the right decision, when she herself was not convinced? Would Daniel even turn up? She grabbed a tissue and blew her nose. Maybe it'd be for the best if he didn't come. That way, she could put off telling them.

She put her bowl of hardly touched spaghetti on the side table and then slumped against the cushions. Was that a coward's way out? Probably. But right then, she didn't care.

～

DANIEL SAT AT THE BAR, cigarette in one hand, a pint in the other. He'd lost count of how many he'd had, and now he didn't care. At one stage, Johnno had encouraged him to go home, but Daniel shook his head and told him he couldn't do it.

"I can't go, Johnny, I just can't. I'm no good for her..." His voice was slurred and his eyes had glazed over. Hunched over his drink, he almost fell off the stool.

"Come over here, then." He looked up as Johnno helped him off the stool and into an alcove.

"What will you tell her?"

Daniel pulled out another cigarette but struggled with his lighter.

"Here, let me help."

Daniel leaned forward and allowed Johnno to light it for him before taking a long drag.

"Dunno mate. But she'll probably throw me out."

～

LIZZY HARDLY SLEPT, drifting in and out of conscious thought and desperate pleas to God. Her anger grew. Anger with herself. With Daniel. With her parents. The very thought of her parents caused heart palpitations. She didn't want to see them.

Sleep must have come at some stage, as daylight peeping through the curtains woke her. Pulling herself up, she looked around. No sign of Daniel. It was cold and empty without him. Where was he? Where had he slept? Was he okay?

She picked up her spaghetti bowl and placed it in the sink. As she stood gazing out the window, she caressed the small baby bump that had recently appeared and breathed in slowly.

The colourful spring blooms in the garden below caught her eye. Her mother's garden would be in full bloom right now. The garden she loved playing in as a child. Her mother's pride and joy - an award winning garden overflowing with colour and design. A young girl in hot pink lycra jogged past, catching her attention. An elderly couple out for a morning stroll with their equally old overweight labrador made her smile.

Then her gaze was drawn to the spot where hers and Daniel's Ford Escort was normally parked. The spot was empty. She closed her eyes and gripped the bench. *God, I need you today. I know I don't deserve your help, but please help me.*

She turned around and walked to the shower.

LIZZY WAS RELIEVED that Daniel hadn't returned before she left. It made it easier. She dressed herself in a skirt and blouse her parents would approve of, rather than the hippy type clothes they abhorred but she preferred. The little baby bump was hidden, and she hoped she'd put on enough make-up to complete the facade. She glanced at herself in the full length mirror in her bedroom, and was pleased with the transition from Lizzy O'Connor to Elizabeth Walton-Smythe. Before she left, she removed her wedding ring and placed it on her dresser.

She checked her watch and called a taxi. Her heart pounded as it pulled up outside the Grand Hotel. She paid the taxi driver, climbed out, and stood on the pavement. How she wished she was anywhere but here at this very moment. But she had no choice, so she steeled herself and walked towards the entrance of the hotel where she'd agreed to meet them at midday.

It took a moment for her eyes to adjust to the dim lighting inside, but it didn't take her long to find Roger and Gwyneth Walton-Smythe. Seated in overstuffed arm chairs that looked like they'd been there since the hotel opened two hundred years before, her mother's back was rod straight as always, and her father looked every inch the country gentleman in his tweed jacket and highly polished brown leather slip-ons.

She tightened her grip on her handbag and clenched her teeth before stepping forward to join them.

"Mother, Father." She stood before them, her eyes steady and her face expressionless.

"Elizabeth. There you are!" Gwyneth Walton-Smythe stood and smiled warmly at her daughter. She held out her hands.

Lizzy took them and then leaned forward, placing a kiss on her mother's cheek.

Her father had also risen. Lizzy, aware of his eyes on her, turned and looked at him. "Good afternoon, Father."

"Good afternoon, Elizabeth." He nodded at her, but with no welcoming arms, she merely returned his nod.

"I see you're on your own," her mother said. "We had expected to see Daniel with you, from what you said on the telephone."

"Daniel couldn't make it. He sends his apologies."

"That's very good news, Elizabeth. I have no desire ever to see that young man again," her father said. "Let's find our table, shall we?"

He called a waiter, who led them to their table in the restaurant. It was all so formal. Daniel would have been out of his comfort zone here. Just as well he hadn't come. The waiter removed the fourth place setting, and took their orders.

The silence was uncomfortable. It had been over four months since 'that' day. Their telephone conversations during that time had been civil, but now face to face, Lizzy was tempted to speak her mind. But no. She had to maintain the facade for now. It also wouldn't be proper to make a scene here.

"What are you going to Edinburgh for?" she asked instead.

"Your father has some business dealings to attend to, and I thought I would go along for the trip," her mother replied. "It's been a long time since we visited Edinburgh, or been away together, for that matter. We're looking forward to it, aren't we, Roger?" Gwyneth reached out and touched Roger's arm lightly, her eyes seeking his.

Lizzy tilted her head, slightly puzzled. What had she seen in her mother's eyes? Could it be longing?

"Yes. It's a lovely old city, Edinburgh." Roger sipped his wine and looked Lizzy in the eye. "And you, Elizabeth. What are you doing with your life? I believe you're still cohorting with that good for nothing Irishman?"

His eye was cold and piercing, but Lizzy held it for as long as she could. "Yes, Father, Daniel and I are still seeing each other. I'm old enough to make my own decisions as to who I see and associate with. If I choose to 'cohort' with Daniel, you will just have to accept that." Her heart pounded in her chest, and she couldn't believe she'd just said that, but it gave her strength to continue.

"You're wasting your life with him, Elizabeth. You could have done so well for yourself. Terence Allsopp still asks after you. He'd marry you tomorrow, I'm sure."

"I'm not interested in Terence Allsopp or any other high-browed son of the well-to-do, Father. You know that." Lizzy's muscles tensed, and she fought hard to control her anger.

"Be it on your own head, then, is all I'll say. I don't know what you see in him."

Lizzy held her retort as the waiter arrived with their meals. Her mother had ordered fish, and the smell of it immediately made her nauseous. She took a sip of her water. *Oh God, please help me control this.* She herself had ordered the simplest, blandest item on the menu. A chicken sandwich.

"Aren't you hungry, Elizabeth?" her mother asked a few minutes later. Lizzy's sandwich lay there, barely touched.

"Please excuse me," she said as she stood. She placed her

napkin neatly on the table, and then walked briskly to the bathroom, hoping she'd make it.

~

"I'M CONCERNED FOR HER, Roger. She doesn't look well." Gwyneth said to Roger once Lizzy had left the table.

"It's hanging around with that lout that's doing it." His eyes narrowed and he breathed heavily. "I've a good mind to find him and give him a piece of my mind."

"You can't do that, Roger. As much as we don't like him, Elizabeth obviously does. Perhaps in time she'll come to her senses. We can only hope." She reached out and touched his arm. "Don't be too hard on her, Roger. We don't want to lose her."

Roger Walton-Smythe looked into his wife's eyes. Maybe she was right. Elizabeth was their only daughter, after all. Such high hopes he'd held for her when she was younger. He'd pictured her riding at Royal Windsor, graduating from Oxford University with Honours, and marrying Terence Allsopp. But now... now... He shook his head and looked away.

~

"ARE YOU ALRIGHT, DEAR?" Gwyneth asked when Lizzy returned.

Lizzy had tried to freshen herself as best she could, but how much longer could she keep it up? She took her seat and placed her napkin on her lap. "Yes, Mother. I'm fine, thank you." Picking up her sandwich, she forced herself to take a bite.

When she looked up, she followed the direction of her mother's eyes and froze. They were fixated on her left hand. *A ring mark.* Her body sagged. She slowly lifted her eyes and looked at her mother.

"Elizabeth, please don't tell me you're married," Gwyneth stammered. Lizzy felt so sorry for her mother in that moment. The colour drained out of her mother's face, and Lizzy feared she might faint.

But Lizzy couldn't deny it. She lowered her hand onto her lap and breathed deeply. "I know you'll both be disappointed, but yes, Daniel and I are married. We were going to tell you, but then Daniel couldn't make it..." Her voice trailed off.

Silence sliced the air like a knife. Lizzy's heart pounded in her chest. What would they say?

"Get out of here immediately, Elizabeth! You disgust me!" Her father stood so fast he knocked his chair over. The waiter ran to help, and every diner in the restaurant stopped eating and gaped at the spectacle.

Lizzy looked at her father and rose. His nostrils flared, and his face had reddened.

"Very well, Father. But you might also like to know you're going to be a grandfather." And with that, she spun on her heels and strode out of the restaurant.

~

GWYNETH GASPED at Lizzy's announcement and reached out to her, but it was too late. Lizzy had disappeared out the door.

Gwyneth stood unsteadily and grabbed Roger's arm. "We need to go after her, Roger. We can't just let her go like that."

"I don't know why we should. I don't understand her at all, Gwyneth. Why would she do such a thing?" Roger ran his hands through his hair and paced on the spot.

"For a number of reasons I can think of." Gwyneth took a deep breath and squared her jaw. "Pay the bill, Roger, then we'll go look for her."

Roger's eyes darted around the restaurant. The others diners had resumed eating and talking, almost as if nothing had happened. He straightened his jacket, lifted his chin, and paid the bill.

Outside the hotel, Roger and Gwyneth stood together on the pavement, their eyes scouring the immediate area for any sign of Lizzy.

"She can't have gone far. Maybe she's in the park," Gwyneth said, pointing across the road.

Roger looked at his watch and drew in a long breath.

Gwyneth stared at him. "How dare you, Roger! She's your daughter. And she's pregnant. We might not like it, but if we don't want to lose her completely, we need to find her."

Roger narrowed his eyes and pursed his lips, but followed Gwyneth across the road.

"I think I see her." Gwyneth grabbed Roger's arm and pulled him along the path to the right to where Lizzy sat on a park bench.

～

LIZZY'S HEAD hung low with her arms wrapped around her stomach. She looked up as her parents came to a standstill in front of her.

55

"I won't talk unless you're civil." She crossed her arms pertly and pulled herself up.

"We'll try, Elizabeth. We'll try." Gwyneth sat beside her daughter and placed her arm gently around Lizzy's shoulder.

Lizzy fought the impulse to pull away, but remained still.

"Are you really expecting?" Gwyneth's voice was surprisingly soothing, and her touch calming. Lizzy hadn't been this close to her mother for many years. Her perfume was still the same. Chanel No. 5. It's distinct, fresh smell evoked so many memories. But right now it made her queasy. She tilted her face slightly to her mother's as she inched away and nodded, her eyes glistening.

Tears rolled down Gwyneth's cheeks. How long had it been since she'd seen her mother cry? Lizzy fetched a tissue from her bag and handed it to her.

"I'm sorry, Elizabeth. It's just such a shock." Gwyneth dabbed her eyes and took a deep breath before continuing. She squeezed Lizzy's hand and searched her eyes. "How are you, dear? Are you feeling okay?"

Lizzy inhaled deeply, and blinked back her own tears. She had to remain strong. "Yes, thank you, Mother. I'm keeping reasonably well."

Gwyneth squeezed Lizzy's hand again, a warm smile growing on her face. "We couldn't leave without finding you, Elizabeth."

Gwyneth tilted her head and looked to Roger for support.

The scowl on Roger's face left no doubt about his feelings. "This is a sorry mess you've got yourself into, girl. I assume you married him because he got you pregnant?" He studied Lizzy with thinly veiled disapproval.

Lizzy looked at him and narrowed her eyes.

"No Father. I wasn't pregnant when we married." She straightened her shoulders defensively. "In fact, you might be surprised to learn I was unblemished when we married."

"I find that hard to believe." Roger turned his back and folded his arms, his head lifted high and his back as straight as a rod.

"Believe it or not, it's true." Lizzy stood and spoke to her father's back, hands defiantly placed on her hips. "I also happen to love Daniel. I don't care what you think, Father, but Daniel and I are married, and we are having a child. Deal with it in whatever way you see fit." She turned and looked at her mother, her demeanour softening. "Mother, I hope you're happy about the news. I'm sure you'll be a wonderful grand-mother." Lizzy smiled warmly at her and then took a deep breath.

Gwyneth returned Lizzy's smile, and wiped another tear from her eye. She reached out her hand to Lizzy. Lizzy took it and squeezed it before walking off. In that moment, Lizzy knew she had an ally in her mother.

CHAPTER 7

*L*izzy hailed a taxi and climbed in. Having snatched one last look at her parents before turning the corner, she settled herself into the back seat and took stock of the turn of events. The words she'd spoken to her father played on her mind. Yes, she was married to Daniel, and they were having a child together. But did she *really* love him?

Moments passed, her mind racing through endless scenarios. Was she with him only because she had no choice now they were having a child? If she did have a choice, would she choose to stay and love him? Or would she still choose Mathew over Daniel if there was the slightest possibility of that happening?

Finally, Lizzy acknowledged she did love him. They weren't just words she'd spat at her father. It was the truth. She loved Daniel, and she'd defend him against her father time and time again.

If only he wouldn't drink.

WHEN LIZZY ENTERED THE APARTMENT, she sighed and trudged to her bedroom. She threw her bag on the bed, walked to the dresser and picked up her wedding ring. Just a simple gold band, yet it tied her to Daniel, for better, for worse. It had also given her secret away. She slipped it onto her finger and held it up.

When would he come home? How she needed his arms around her.

HER BODY TENSED when she heard the key turn in the lock. Sleep had eluded her once again, and she glanced at the clock, even though she already knew it was past midnight. Where had he been all this time?

She jumped as one of his boots flew off and hit the wall. He lumbered into the bedroom and undressed clumsily. The stench of alcohol permeated the room and made her nauseous. She remained still but her heart beat fast. *Oh God, please protect me.* She tensed when he climbed into bed, but relaxed a little as he settled in close to her and wrapped his arm gently around her. His body shuddered as he wept. She rolled over and hugged him.

LIZZY ROSE EARLY despite the late night. She glanced at Daniel sleeping soundly, and tip-toed out of the room so as not to wake him. Standing in the kitchen, waiting for the kettle to boil, she picked up one of their few framed wedding photos.

How much had changed since that day when she so naively married him.

The kettle whistled and she poured herself a cup of tea. Sitting on the couch, she glanced at her Bible laying unopened and neglected on the side table. She picked it up and opened it, the familiar feel of the pages warming her heart. *It's been too long, Lord. Please forgive me.*

Lizzy flicked through several pages before settling on Psalm 42, one of her favourites. She read the words before humming them, and as she sang, tears streamed down her face. *'Yes Lord, as the deer pants for the water, so my soul longs after you. You alone are my heart's desire and I long to worship you. You alone are my strength, my shield, to you alone will my spirit yield. You alone are my heart's desire and I long to worship you.'*

Closing her eyes, Lizzy prayed for forgiveness for marrying Daniel while she still loved Mathew. She prayed for Daniel, that he'd come to know God's love in his life, and that he'd learn to face his problems without the need for alcohol. For their baby, that it would be healthy and strong, and wrapped in love. For her parents and their relationship. And for herself.

Lizzy felt God's presence in the very depths of her soul. She felt renewed, refreshed.

The alarm brought her back to the present. She jumped up and ran to the bedroom to turn it off, but she was too slow - Daniel was awake and pulling himself up as she entered the room. The smell of stale alcohol made her gag, and she brought her hand to her mouth.

She stopped and looked at him. His eyes were bleary and he needed a wash and a shave. Lizzy bit her lip and decided there and then, she'd love him as she'd promised...

He leaned against the pillows and looked at her with sorrow in his eyes. "Lizzy, come here my sweet girl. I'm sorry."

She walked to the bed and climbed into his arms. He kissed the top of her head and pulled her tight.

THEY SAT at the table and shared the breakfast Lizzy had prepared. Not that she ate much, but she needed to be near him. She leaned back in her chair and studied the outline of his face, wondering at the turn of events that resulted in her sitting here with him like this. Eventually she spoke the words he had to hear.

"They know, Daniel. My parents know about us and the baby."

His hand stopped midway to his mouth and his eyes widened.

"Oh….. Lizzy, I'm so sorry." He lowered his fork and reached his hand out to her. The genuine sorrow in his eyes touched her heart. "Tell me what happened."

As she told him about the meeting with her parents, the need to discuss his actions of the week leading up to it pressed on her. It couldn't just be ignored. It was wrong of him to have left her to face her parents on her own. He was her husband, and he should have been there to support her. Instead, where was he? She could get really angry if she wasn't careful. Maybe she needed to. Just because she loved him, it didn't mean he could get away with treating her like this.

She swallowed before looking him in the eye.

"Daniel, we need to talk about why you weren't there."

He looked startled and didn't answer straight away. His

body was rigid, she'd rattled him. She didn't care. They had to talk about it.

Lizzy's gaze remained on Daniel. Silence filled the air with only the ticking of the clock interrupting it.

He put his toast down and folded his arms before finally responding. "I know I let you down this week, Lizzy, and I feel bad about it." He sighed wearily and lifted his eyes. "I'm sorry. I should have been there." He took her hand and looked into her eyes. "I promise I'll never let you down again."

Lizzy thought for a moment. He'd apologised, but could she trust him? She tilted her head and tapped her fingers on the table.

"That's a big promise, Daniel. What makes you think you can keep it, when every day this week you said you were sorry after you'd been out drinking, but then you still did it again?" She straightened her head and regarded him with a steady gaze. "I don't see that anything's changed, really."

He sighed and dipped his head, his whole body slumping. "You're right, Lizzy. It was the thought of seeing your parents. It was just easier to drink and disappear than face them."

"Well, that's a start, I guess. But it doesn't excuse your behaviour. You let me down, Daniel." She sat back and crossed her arms pertly, almost savouring his discomfort. "I hope next time we have a difficult situation you'll be man enough to face it."

Lizzy's eyes were unwavering. Daniel averted his face and stared out the window. Had she said too much? Her heart thumped in her chest.

At last he turned back and let out a long, low sigh.

"I don't know, Lizzy. All I can do is try."

Lizzy eased off just a little. Really, that was all she could ask for. "Well, you need to try hard, Daniel. For the baby's sake, and mine." She stood and placed her hands on the back of the chair. "I'm going to church today. Maybe you should come with me." She walked to the sink and began washing the dishes.

DANIEL REMAINED SEATED. His head hurt, but Lizzy's words had hurt him more. He didn't want to lose her. He loved her too much. But could he go to church? Maybe he needed to.

He closed his eyes and leaned on his elbows. What kind of a man was he to let his wife go through what Lizzy had just gone through? He really was no good for her. But he loved her.

He stood and walked to the bedroom.

"Wait, Liz, I'll come with you."

LIZZY PEERED from the bathroom to where Daniel was seated on the bed, slipping his boots on. She'd been wondering as she got ready if he'd come. Maybe God was answering her prayers already.

She looked at him and smiled, and sent up a quick prayer of thanks.

Standing in church a little while later with Daniel beside her, Lizzy felt at peace. Ever since she'd committed her heart to the Lord when she was at University with Sal, she'd loved going to church. Sure, she knew God was with her constantly,

63

and she could pray to Him wherever she was, but there was something special about joining together with other believers in praise and worship. And she'd really missed it. But now, it was like the Holy Spirit was breathing new life into her heart.

She prayed that Daniel would also feel God reaching out to him, and that his heart would be open. It would be so wonderful if they could be on the same path. Marrying Daniel when he didn't share her faith was just another mistake on her part, so now she needed to trust God to work it out for them. It did make her wonder, however, how many of her mistakes she could expect God to fix up. Was it presumptuous of her to ask God to fix the situations she'd got herself into? Time to think more about later. For now, she would just enjoy being in God's house. She squeezed Daniel's hand as they took their seats, and snuggled closer to him.

At the end of the service Nessa came over and hugged her. It'd been a while since they'd seen each other, and Lizzy chastised herself for letting their friendship slip. It was Nessa, after all, who'd introduced her to Daniel. It crossed her mind that Nessa most likely knew about Daniel and his drinking.

When Nessa invited them to lunch the following Sunday, it gave the perfect opportunity to talk to her about him.

CHAPTER 8

*T*he week passed without event, much to Lizzy's relief. She did, however, check the clock every few minutes from about four o'clock onwards, and often jumped up to look out the classroom window to see if Daniel had arrived. She knew she was being overly anxious, as he'd promised he'd be there by half four. So far he'd arrived on time or early every day.

When half four came on Friday and he wasn't there, she started to panic. She was packed and ready to go, so she locked the classroom door and headed out to the car park. She bit on her lip as she walked to the wall where she'd sat so often the previous week. She sat down, but stood again straight away. *I'm **not** going to do this. I said I wouldn't wait.* She sighed and clenched her fists. *Oh God, where is he?* She walked to the edge of the road. The angrier she became, the faster her heart beat. She'd just put her hand out to hail a taxi when she saw the Ford Escort trundling along the road towards her.

She let out a huge sigh, and shook her head at Daniel as he pulled up.

He leaned over and opened the door. "Sorry sweetie. The traffic was worse today." He kissed her as she sat beside him. Why had she doubted him?

GWYNETH CALLED THAT NIGHT. Lizzy took the phone and sat on the couch. Daniel was still eating his dinner, but he shifted his chair so he could see her face.

"Mother, how was your trip?"

"Edinburgh was lovely, dear. And your father's business dealings were successful. But how are you? How is your morning sickness?"

"Not so bad this week. I've been feeling better most days, thanks."

"Your news surprised us, Elizabeth, I have to say. We'd certainly never expected it."

"I'm sorry I shocked you, Mother. I hope Father will come around."

"He'd like a word, if that's okay."

Lizzy's chest tightened. She glanced at Daniel before answering. "Okay. Put him on."

"Elizabeth."

"Father."

"Elizabeth, as your mother said, your news shocked us." He paused. "Your mother and I have been talking. We don't approve of your choice. I dare say we never will, however, you are our only daughter, and we would like to give you a proper wedding. Please think about it."

Lizzy's eyes widened and she stared at Daniel, unable to speak.

"Elizabeth, did you hear me?"

"Ah, yes, Father. You took me by surprise this time. I'm not sure what to say. I'll need to discuss it with Daniel."

"Very well, then. I guess that was to be expected. You'll need to think about it quickly, given your condition. Good-bye, Elizabeth."

"Good-bye, Father."

Lizzy placed the receiver on the hook and leaned back on the couch, deep in thought. Daniel joined her. "What did he say?"

She took a deep breath and looked at him. His eyebrows were drawn together and his gaze intense. "Father and Mother would like to give us a proper wedding."

His mouth gaped. "You mean, with all the bells and whistles?" Lizzy nodded. "Forget it. I'm not going to be paraded around for his benefit. That's all he'd be doing it for. To save face. I'm sorry, Lizzy, I can't do it." He shook his head vehemently.

Lizzy wasn't sure what she wanted. She'd always dreamt of a fairytale wedding, especially when she thought she'd be marrying Mathew Carter. It was tempting. But Daniel was probably right. Father wouldn't be offering this for their benefit. And she wouldn't want to expose Daniel to all the dramas of a society wedding, with all its snobbery and melodrama. No, she didn't want this either.

"It's okay, Daniel. I'll say no."

He hugged her and whispered in her ear, "I love you, Elizabeth O'Connor."

They remained in each other's arms for several minutes before Daniel pulled away. "Let's go out, Lizzy. Let's go dancing."

Her eyes lit up and her smile broadened to a grin. "That would be lovely, Daniel!"

"It's wonderful to be out, Daniel. I'd started thinking my dancing days were over," Lizzy whispered into Daniel's ear as he led her around the dance floor of the Mariat Hotel.

"We need to do it more often, while I can still get my arm around you."

She threw her head back and laughed. "I can't say I'm looking forward to being fat."

"You'll look beautiful, Mrs O'Connor." Daniel leaned forward and planted a kiss on her cheek.

The music picked up, and they transitioned easily into a jive. Lizzy didn't care they were being watched. She was out with Daniel, and she was going to enjoy herself.

"I think I need to sit," she said breathlessly when the music finally stopped.

Daniel helped her to a seat. "I'm sorry, Lizzy. That was stupid," he said as he poured her a glass of water.

Lizzy took a gulp before looking at him. "But it was fun." She laughed and her eyes twinkled.

"Yes, it was fun." He leaned back and smiled at her.

"Let's take a walk, Daniel. I'm not ready to go home yet." Lizzy stood and took his arm, and led him outside towards the river. She clung to him, breathing in his manly scent - a mixture of sweat, after-shave, and cigarette smoke. The intoxicating mix sent a shiver through her body.

"Are you cold?" Daniel wrapped his arm around her and pulled her close.

She looked up at him, her eyes full of love. "No. It's just what you do to me."

He spun her around and looked deeply into her eyes before he kissed her.

"Maybe we should go home." His breath on hers was warm and inviting.

"Not yet," she whispered. "Let's walk a little further."

She leaned close as they strolled along the path. *If only this night could go on forever.* She squeezed his arm and when he kissed the top of her head, Lizzy thought she was in heaven.

"Let's never have a week like last week ever again," she said as she leaned her head on his shoulder.

THE FLASHING NEON lights ahead caught her attention. "Oh look, Daniel, an ice-cream stand! Can we get one?"

"Of course, sweet girl."

As they sat on a bench watching the boats puttering up and down the river, licking their ice-creams, Lizzy turned her head and asked Daniel in a soft voice, "Why did you decide to come to church with me last Sunday?"

Daniel stopped mid lick. "Where did that come from?"

"It's just been on my mind this week, that's all. You said you didn't like going, so I'm curious about the change of heart."

Daniel slumped on the bench. Her question had thrown him. Maybe she shouldn't have asked.

He sighed heavily. "I'm not sure, Lizzy. It was a spur of the moment decision. I think I just wanted to be with you." He pulled her close and hugged her.

Lizzy leaned her head on his shoulder, her heart fallen. That wasn't the answer she'd hoped for.

CHAPTER 9

"*D*on't forget Nessa asked us to lunch today," Lizzy said as she climbed out of bed the following Sunday morning. "Are you coming to Church again?"

Daniel rolled over and stared out the window while she stood waiting for his answer.

"It's okay, you don't have to come. No pressure." *But God, I pray he will.*

She jumped into the shower and while she washed her hair she prayed. *'What a week, Lord. I'm so glad we're back on talking terms. Please be with Daniel. I know he's got stuff going on inside. He needs you, Lord. I don't know what's worrying him, but he needs to let go of whatever it is. Please help him. And help me to help him too. And please can you help my parents, especially my father, accept our situation? And lastly, Lord God, bless this little baby. Keep him or her safe and well. Thank you Lord God for this day and for loving me.'*

She caressed her tummy and began to hum, allowing the

Spirit to cleanse her soul while the warm water cleansed her body.

LIZZY SMILED when she re-entered the bedroom. Daniel was up and dressed and looking as charming as ever.

"I guess you're coming, then?

"Yes, I'm coming. I can't let you go on your own. Too many single men prowling around."

Lizzy's heart fell a little. "Well that's an interesting reason for going to church. I don't think any man would be interested in me if they knew my condition, though." She looked down at her baby belly which was still barely noticeable.

"Lizzy, any man would find you attractive, regardless of your condition."

"Are you flirting with me, Daniel O'Connor?"

"Maybe." She shook her head when he winked at her.

SITTING in church a little while later, Lizzy looked around and saw her good friends, Colin and Linda, and also Nessa and Riley. Two people she didn't know sat beside them. She guessed they were Nessa's brother and sister. Having just sung an old hymn and holding Daniel's hand, her heart was full. She turned her head and smiled at him. *Mmm, I could easily get used to this.* God had a lot of work to do, both in her own life, and in Daniel's, but it was a start, and for that she was thankful.

"IT SEEMS a long time since we met at Nessa's party," Lizzy said to Daniel in the car on the way to Nessa and Riley's a little while later.

"I'm glad you were there, Liz. You captured my heart the moment I saw you." He glanced at her and winked.

She laughed at him. He was so easy to love when he was like this. Playful and funny. Easy to get on with. She leaned back in her seat and relaxed. *But how long will it last if he doesn't deal with whatever's worrying him?*

For now, she would just enjoy the moment, and leave the rest to God.

"NESSA, THANKS FOR INVITING US!" Lizzy said as Nessa hugged her and showed her and Daniel into their living room.

"A pleasure, Lizzy. It's good to see you both. And you're looking well. As are you, Daniel."

Lizzy couldn't help but notice the look that passed between the two of them. *I need that talk with her. See if she can fill me in on anything I should know.*

"Come and meet my sister, Lizzy. She's visiting with my brother for a week. I think you'll like her." And with that, Nessa drew Lizzy away from Daniel.

Lizzy's mind wasn't on what Nessa or her sister, Fiona, were saying. She was focused on what Daniel was saying to Riley, and hoped she replied appropriately at the right times.

She held her breath when she overheard Daniel asking Riley for a beer. *Why is he asking for a beer? He hasn't had a drink for a whole week.* Her body relaxed a little at Riley's reply.

"Why don't we just stick to the soft stuff today?"

But then she could have throttled Daniel when he pressed Riley further.

"Oh, come on Riley. What's wrong with you? Just get a man a beer will you?"

She stared at Daniel, not caring if Nessa or her sister saw her. Lizzy's body tensed as Daniel walked to the refrigerator and helped himself to a beer.

"Are you okay, Lizzy?" Nessa asked. "Do you want to sit down? You're looking very pale all of a sudden."

Lizzy quickly turned back to Nessa and Fiona. "Sorry Nessa. I'm fine. I was just a little distracted. Where were we?"

"I was just saying we should go for a girls' night out while Fiona's here. Are you up for that?"

"Ah...I guess so. Depends on when." She glanced at Daniel before continuing. "I've got a busy week at school, but I'll see if I can make it."

Daniel had been joined by the man who'd sat beside Nessa in church, who she assumed was Nessa's brother. Nothing tangible, but a bad feeling settled in her stomach.

"Can I help you with lunch, Nessa?" Lizzy asked once having pulled herself together. It was only one beer, after all. But it was the way he'd demanded it that concerned her.

"It smells wonderful, Ness. Lasagne and garlic bread. Lovely!"

"Yes. It's Fiona and Liam's favourite. Some help would be good, thanks Liz. Your morning sickness must be better?"

"Mainly. I still get a little queasy now and then, but much better than a few weeks ago. Where are your two, by the way?"

"Oh, they're in their rooms. Liam brought them over some new games. They haven't stopped playing with them since."

Nessa put the tray of vegetables back in the oven after checking them, and then stood with her arms folded, looking at Lizzy. "So how are things really, Liz? Has Daniel been behaving himself?"

Lizzy looked up, trying not to look startled. How much should she say? Should she tell her everything? Maybe not. Not the time or the place, anyway. But then, Nessa obviously knew more than she was letting on. And she did want to talk to her. She sighed heavily and looked away.

"Please tell me he's not mistreating you."

Lizzy turned her head back with a surprised look on her face. "No. He hasn't been perfect, put it that way, but he hasn't mistreated me. He's been great this past week." She paused, and took a deep breath. "Not so good the week before. My parents stopped in last Saturday, and I think he was anxious about it. So was I, to tell the truth."

"Mmm. He's never been too good in sticky situations. I'd hoped he'd improved. But you're good for him, Lizzy. And he loves you. You can tell just by the way he looks at you. Be patient with him."

Lizzy felt tears well up in her eyes and tried to push them back, but when Nessa walked over and hugged her, they began to fall.

"If ever you want to talk, Liz, just let me know." She pulled her closer and than grabbed some tissues.

"Now, let's get this lunch sorted."

LIZZY SQUEEZED Daniel's hand while Riley gave thanks. Now seated beside him, she could keep an eye on him, and maybe encourage him to stick to the soft stuff. He seemed okay at the moment. Happy and jovial, the life of the party. But maybe it was just a facade, a cover up, and underneath he was actually insecure. *Where did that thought come from?* She looked at him. Was he being slightly louder than normal? *Oh Daniel. What's going on inside you?*

"This is a lovely meal, Nessa," Fiona said. Yes, it was a lovely meal. She should just relax and enjoy the fantastic spread Nessa had prepared, and enjoy being outside on such a lovely summer's day. But something wasn't right. An underlying tension, but she didn't know what was causing it.

"My pleasure, Fiona," Nessa replied. "It's lovely to have you all here. Eat up everyone. There's plenty to go round."

Lizzy began to eat, but looked up when Liam, sitting opposite Daniel, spoke to him directly.

"You haven't properly introduced me to your wife yet, Daniel."

Liam's eyes held a glint. How many had he drunk? More than a few, by the looks of it.

Daniel straightened, his body tense beside her. What would he say? His words played back in her mind. Was he thinking that Liam was one of those prowling single men he meant to protect her from?

"Liam, this is Elizabeth, my wife." Their eyes locked. "Keep your hands off," Daniel leaned forward and hissed.

Lizzy stiffened as everyone stared at Daniel.

Riley broke the silence. "Come on everyone. Don't let Nessie's good food go to waste. Eat up."

Lizzy breathed a sigh of relief when Daniel picked up his fork and began to eat.

"DANIEL, we need to go. I've got preparation to do for tomorrow." He was swaying. How many had he had? She'd only left him on his own while she helped with the dishes, but he must have downed one after the other in quick succession if his demeanour was anything to go by. A sickness developed in the pit of Lizzy's stomach.

"Just let me finish this one, Lizzy love." He draped his arm around her shoulder and pulled her close. She resisted him, and instead sent him an unwavering glare.

"I think you've had enough, Daniel," she hissed into his ear. "We need to go." Riley and Liam stood together, watching. She turned her head quickly so they couldn't see her face. "Daniel, we really need to go."

She grabbed his arm. It was going to be awkward. She guided Daniel towards the gate, and called out to Nessa through the door as they passed. Riley offered to help, but she thanked him and continued on her own.

Lizzy directed him into the passenger's seat, although he put up a fight. He wanted to drive, but there was no way she'd let him. Once she'd pulled out onto the road, she turned her head and took a quick look at him. She didn't like what she saw. His whole manner had changed, and she didn't feel comfortable or safe with him. She remained quiet, hoping he'd fall asleep on the way home.

She fought to control her tears. How had this happened? What had gone on between Daniel and Liam? She wanted to shake him. This wasn't her Daniel.

He moved beside her and sat forward. His eyes bored into her. Lizzy gripped the wheel tighter.

"Why d'you make a scene like that for, Lizbeth?" he spat at

her. "Didya want to impress that young cousin of mine? I saw the way he looked at you."

Lizzy glanced at him. His eyes were glazed, and she didn't like the way he was talking.

"Don't talk rot, Daniel. I just needed to get home, you know that." She looked straight ahead, and concentrated on driving, but her heart was racing.

"Tell me what was going on, Lizbeth."

"What do you mean? Where?"

"Don't give me that nonsense," Daniel spat at her.

"I don't know what you mean, Daniel." She tried to remain calm on the outside, but inside her heart pounded.

"I don't believe you." He moved his face closer to hers. "What was going on?"

"With what? I really don't know what you're talking about."

"With that cousin of mine, that's what. I saw the way he looked at you. You stay away from him. I'm warning you."

"You're talking rubbish, Daniel. Nothing was going on." Lizzy gripped the wheel tighter to steady her shaking hands. What had gotten into him? Maybe she should pull over.

Seconds passed. Would he let it go? She daren't look at him. When Daniel at last sat back in his seat, she exhaled slowly.

What had happened to make him act like that? The look in his eyes had scared her. She liked nothing about the Daniel she'd just seen. Tears rolled down her cheeks as she drove the remaining distance home.

LIZZY WAS TEMPTED to leave him asleep in the car when they pulled up outside the apartment a short while later. Her arms slumped over the wheel, she closed her eyes and wiped the tears that had continued to fall. *God, where are you in all of this? I don't know what to do. I don't know how to cope. Please help me.*

Daniel stirred beside her. She sat up and studied his face. Would he remember what had happened? She certainly would. It didn't make any sense at all. What did he think she'd done? What if he did remember and apologised? Could she forgive him again? Should she consider leaving him? But what about her vows? She'd promised to love him, in good times and bad. Even though they hadn't said their vows in a church in front of God, to her it was as if they had. She was married to Daniel, for better or worse. And this was certainly worse. But how could she go on? How could she forgive him? Expecting his baby made it worse. Maybe she should leave for the baby's sake. But no, maybe the baby would help Daniel come to his senses.

Wiping her face, she drew a sober breath, and hung her head. *I don't know I can forgive him, Lord. You've got to help me. I really don't know how to handle this.* She looked at her hands. Their shaking had lessened, but her heart was heavy.

Daniel shifted in his seat and her body tensed. His eyes opened and he turned his head to look at her.

"What are we doing here?"

Lizzy hesitated before answering. It was all too fresh in her mind. It'd be so easy to respond angrily, but then what would he do? She was no match for him. She breathed deeply and stilled herself.

"Waiting for you to wake up. I can't carry you up the stairs."

"Let's go then." His voice still held a slur but had lost a little of its sting. He opened his door, but before he got out, Daniel turned and looked at her with dark eyes. "Stay away from Liam, Elizabeth."

WHEN LIZZY WOKE the following morning, her heart was still heavy. As she'd expected, Daniel apologized and went to bed early, but she had trouble sleeping. She couldn't shake off the utter shock of it all. How could she ever forget? Or forgive?

She sat on the edge of the bed with her head in her hands.

Daniel stirred, and she held her body rigid. She relaxed a little when he seemed to be back to his normal self.

Instead of getting up, Lizzy lay back on the bed and curled up in a ball.

"I don't feel too well, Daniel. I think I'll stay home today." She pulled the bed covers around her and closed her eyes.

"I'll make you a cup of tea, Liz. Stay there. Stay in bed all day if you need."

Tears squeezed their way through her closed eyes and landed on her pillow. How could a person be so different one minute to the next?

When he left for work, she reached for the phone and made a call.

"Nessa, can we go for coffee today?"

CHAPTER 10

*a*n hour later, Lizzy sat opposite Nessa. Once she'd made up her mind to make the call, her body had responded and she felt better immediately. The hope that she might gain some insight into his past spurred her on.

"I'm glad you could make it, Nessa. And at short notice. I hope Fiona didn't mind you going out without her?"

"No, she had some things to do today, so no problem." Nessa looked at her intently. "I assume this is about Daniel?"

Lizzy nodded and lowered her eyes.

"I had hoped he'd sorted himself out. But seems not."

"I need to know about him, Nessa." Lizzy looked up and leaned forward. "I need to know what makes him tick. He won't tell me much about his past. Just snippets here and there." She took in a deep breath and sipped her coffee. "I'm not coping too well with his changing moods. Sometimes he can be so loving and kind, and other times he can be so horrible. Usually when he's been drinking." *Like yesterday on the way*

81

home. She glanced outside and saw people scurrying in the rain. The sun had definitely gone.

When Nessa squeezed her hand, Lizzy struggled to hold back her tears.

"You poor girl. He should be treating you like a precious princess. I know he loves you, but yes, he does have a past, Lizzy." Nessa's eyes bore into hers. "Do you really want to know?"

Lizzy nodded, her eyes unmoving.

"Daniel's one of eight children. The second eldest. I assume you know that already?"

Lizzy nodded again.

"His father drank heavily, and treated his mother badly. It wasn't uncommon in our area of Belfast. His father disappeared when he was ten, leaving his mother to bring up the children on her own. She always made sure they were well dressed and went to church. She did the best she could." Nessa stopped and took another sip of her coffee.

"His mother, my aunt, got sick a few years later. She died of cancer not long after, and the kids were all split up. Daniel came to live with us." *Come on Nessa, I know all of this. Move on.*

"Everything was fine for the first few years, but you could tell he was angry about losing his mother. He wouldn't go to church with us. He said he blamed God for letting her die. He was a bit younger than me, and I kept a look out for him. He was always loud, funny and charming. Just like he is now most of the time. He hasn't lost that. But when he was sixteen, he started drinking. It was the done thing. Most of the lads did it. We all knew, but couldn't do anything to stop it. One night he got so drunk he ended up in hospital. My parents told him if he didn't stop, he'd have to leave. They didn't want him setting a bad example for my brothers." She paused before continuing and glanced out the window. "He agreed to stop, but they also said he needed to go to church with them if he wanted to stay. He reluctantly agreed, and that's where he met Ciara."

Lizzy leaned forward and rested on her elbows. "This is the bit I don't know. He never talks about her to me."

"I'm not surprised," Nessa said. "The whole thing messed him up pretty badly." She leaned forward, their heads almost touching. "Ciara was lovely. They were inseparable, but he got her pregnant. He was seventeen, and she was sixteen. Her parents were shocked. They were good Christian people, and they thought she was too. My parents were more angry than shocked. They made him marry her, even though they were so young. They lived in the back room of our house. They didn't have any money. Daniel tried to find work, but could only get the odd job here and there. Not enough to support a family."

Nessa leaned back and crossed her arms.

"I feel bad making you remember all of this, Nessa." Lizzy reached out and squeezed her hand. "Are you okay?"

She met Lizzy's gaze. "Yes, I'm fine. It's just a sad story, that's all." She took a deep breath. "The baby was born. It was a little girl. They called her Rachel, and she was perfect. Daniel was a changed person. He doted on her, and being a father made him grow up. He got a job, and they moved into their own place. Everything was perfect until the night Rachel died in her sleep. There was no real explanation. Just 'cot death'.

"Daniel began drinking again. He lost his job, and often he wouldn't come home for days on end." Nessa leaned forward and sighed. "One night when he did come home, Liam was there. He had his arms around Ciara, and she was crying on his shoulder. Daniel grabbed him and punched him. He punched him until Liam could hardly move. He probably would have killed him if Ciara hadn't hit him with a saucepan."

Lizzy's eyes widened and her body slumped a little.

"She didn't want to call the police, but Liam was hurt so badly he needed to go to hospital. Daniel was charged with assault, and he was sent to jail for twelve months."

"Oh goodness, Nessa. I had no idea." Lizzy's mind reeled with this information. She rubbed her temple with her fingers and then looked up. "What happened to Liam?"

"He had some broken ribs, and was covered in bruises. He recovered."

"So was he with Ciara, or did Daniel get it wrong?"

"Liam said he'd just gone round there to see Daniel, and found Ciara crying. No-one really knows apart from him. He maintains they weren't together."

"What happened to her?"

Nessa sighed sadly. "She went back home to live with her parents. She was never the same though." Nessa brushed tears away from her eyes and gulped. "She took her life a few years later. Her family was devastated. They blamed Daniel. They still do."

Lizzy grabbed Nessa's hand. "That's a terrible story, Nessa. No wonder he doesn't want to talk about it. But now I understand why he acted like he did yesterday."

Nessa pulled out a tissue and blew her nose. "Yes, well. He shouldn't have been drinking, that's for sure." She inhaled deeply and checked her watch. "There's more. Have you got time?"

"I have if you have. Do you want another coffee?"

"Yes please."

Lizzy called the waiter over and ordered two more coffees. "Okay, tell me the rest."

"When Daniel got out of jail, he was a mess. He went straight back onto the bottle and almost drank himself to death. We were all worried about him, but there wasn't much anyone could do. One night he got picked up by the Salvos. They took him to a home and cared for him. He must have been really bad, because they convinced him to get help. He started going to AA. It worked for a while. We couldn't believe it was the same person when we saw him a few months later. It was like having the old Daniel back, but better. He patched it up with Liam, and apologised for beating him up. That was five years ago.

"By that time I'd married Riley. We moved over here not long after, so I didn't see much of him after that, but I heard he was doing well most of the time. He got himself a job at the hospital, but then all of a sudden he just packed up and disappeared. The next thing I know, he's knocking on our door several years later. He said he needed to get out of the place. Too many memories, and so he went travelling, as you know. He went lots of places, and got jobs where he could. I think he might have been drunk a lot of the time, because he can't remember much about the places he went to."

The waiter arrived with their coffees and Lizzy thanked him.

"When he arrived on our doorstep, it seemed he was ready to settle down. We took him in, on the condition he didn't drink. He was older, obviously, but he also seemed more mature. He wouldn't come to church with us, though. Seemed like he still blamed God for both his mother's and Rachel's deaths. And Ciara's too, for that matter. But apart from that, he seemed to have sorted himself out. He got the job at the hospital, and he wasn't drinking. And then, that's when he met you."

Lizzy sat back in her seat and took a few moments to digest all of this information. She glanced out the window. It was still raining. She turned and looked at Nessa. "Why didn't you tell me any of this before, Ness?"

Nessa held her eyes for a moment, but then looked away. She took a deep breath before answering. "I guess because you seemed so happy together. We didn't really expect it to get so serious so quickly, but by the time it did, it was too late. We just hoped and prayed he was a changed man, and that he'd look after you properly. We assumed he'd tell you in his own time. But obviously, he didn't."

"Why did you ask us over yesterday when you knew Liam would be there?"

"They've seen each other a few times since that day, Liz. Daniel apologised, as I said before, and they haven't had any problems that I know of since. We had no reason to think it would cause a problem." She stopped and tilted her head, her eyes narrowing. "Did something happen last night?"

Lizzy looked her in the eye. *Do I tell her, or do I just let it pass?*

"Not really. He was just a little agitated for a while."

"I'm glad. I didn't realize he'd drunk so much until after you'd left. Too busy with cooking I suppose. I'm sure he'll be fine, Lizzy. Especially with the baby coming. He really does love you."

"I think I need some time alone, Ness."

Nessa's head shot up, her eyes wide open.

"Oh, I don't mean, go away, if that's what you're thinking. I meant now. I think I need to go for a walk, even though it's raining." Lizzy glanced outside again. The rain had stopped, but the sky was still grey. "I need to gather my thoughts. Knowing this puts a whole different slant on everything."

"I understand, Lizzy. It's a lot to take in. I'm sorry I didn't tell you earlier." Nessa reached out and squeezed Lizzy's hand. "I really am." She looked into Lizzy's eyes. "Would it have made a difference if I had?"

Lizzy leaned back and folded her arms and thought for a moment before answering.

"I don't know. But it's irrelevant now. I married him."

She looked up when the waiter came over and asked if they'd like another drink.

"No, but thanks for asking. We're just about to leave."

Lizzy stood and straightened her skirt. "Thanks for coming, Nessa. And for sharing. Now I've got to process it."

Nessa hugged her. "God bless you, Lizzy."

They walked out together. Lizzy shivered.

"Here, take my jacket if you're going to walk."

Lizzy smiled at her. "Thanks Ness."

LIZZY TURNED LEFT and crossed the road. It wasn't raining as such, but a fine mist had settled in the air. Although it was refreshing, she slipped Nessa's jacket on anyway. She didn't want to get sick on top of everything else. She walked along the river, unaware of the activity carrying on either side of her, both on the water and on the road. Lizzy's mind was in turmoil. She'd never dreamt that Daniel could have been hiding so much of himself from her. Why hadn't he told her? Weren't husbands and wives supposed to share everything with each other and not keep secrets? How could she have been so naive when she married him? She'd jumped blindly into marriage with a man she hardly knew anything about. *Was I really that desperate?*

She kept walking, but couldn't get the picture of Daniel being in jail out of her mind. *Jail?* What would her parents say if they ever found out? And poor Ciara. She must have been so brokenhearted and depressed to have taken her own life. Lizzy stopped and sat on a bench seat and bowed her head.

Oh God. This is too much to bear. No wonder Daniel's in turmoil most of the time. He needs you, Lord. Really needs you. Only you can take his hurt and anger away. He needs to forgive himself, Lord. He's been through so much. Please touch him in a special way today. And show me how to love him. Really love him.

An image of a dove settling on her shoulder flitted through her mind and peace flooded through her being. She also knew what she must do.

CHAPTER 11

*L*izzy stepped back to inspect her handiwork and smiled. The table looked perfect. And the smell of roast chicken made her feel hungry. How good it was not to feel queasy anymore. She was just unsure about how to broach the subject with Daniel. Should she just come straight out and tell him she knew everything? That she'd plied the information from Nessa, or should she press him to tell her, and not let on she already knew? Either way was fraught with danger.

Lord God, you need to be with me in this. It could go really well, or it could end really badly. Please give me wisdom.

She glanced out the window. The car wasn't there yet. *What if he doesn't come home?* Lizzy rubbed the back of her neck and breathed deeply. Checking the table once more, she adjusted the small bunch of daisies she'd picked on the way home, and then looked at her watch. *Where is he?*

She'd just about given up hope when she heard the key in

the door. Her body tensed. He was an hour late. Did that mean he'd been drinking? His treatment of her in the car the previous afternoon was still fresh in her mind. She looked up as he entered, and sent up a silent prayer of thanks when he appeared to be sober.

Lizzy stood slowly, and walked over to him. Lifting her arms, she wrapped them around him and caressed his back, then pulled away slightly so she could look at him.

"Daniel O'Connor, I love you." Then she kissed him.

"Jaysus woman! What are you trying to do to me?"

"Shh! And don't swear…"

She led him to the bedroom and made love to him.

"I DON'T KNOW what got into you, Liz, but if this is what a day at home does to you, maybe you should stay at home more often." Daniel rolled over and looked deeply into Lizzy's eyes. "I don't know what I did to deserve you, Elizabeth O'Connor, but I'm very glad you're my wife." He kissed her gently, and then pulled her close. "I'm sorry for yesterday, Lizzy. Forgive me?"

She nodded, her face expanding into a beaming grin before she planted another kiss on his lips.

"COME ON THEN, dinner will be ruined if we don't get up and eat," Lizzy said as she sat up and pulled on her loose fitting shift.

"It smells great, Liz. I could eat a horse after that frolic!"

She led him to the table, and dished out the roast chicken

and vegetables she'd prepared earlier. She lit the candles, and then sat and took his hand.

"Daniel, will you give thanks tonight?"

He squeezed her hand and then he prayed. She wiped tears away with her other hand as she listened to his words that for once sounded genuine.

"This is grand, Lizzy. Thank you," he said as he picked up his knife and fork and began to eat.

Now the time had come, she hesitated. What if he thought she'd just done all of this to trick him, to lure him into talking about his past? No, she couldn't think like that. She'd been genuine in her loving. Surely he would know that. She played with her food a little, and then took a deep breath.

"Daniel, I had coffee with Nessa today. I asked her to tell me about what happened with Ciara and Liam."

His hand stopped midway to his mouth. He turned his head and stared at her.

Her heart thumped. *Oh God, here we go...*

He put his fork down and leaned back in his seat.

Lizzy reached over and touched his hand. "Please Daniel. Don't be upset. It was time I knew, don't you think?"

"Is that what this is about?" He indicated to the plates on the table and narrowed his eyes.

She sighed in frustration and shook her head. "Daniel. We're married, for better or worse. I don't want it to get worse, but it might if we're not honest with each other. I know you'd rather try to ignore what happened, but seeing you with Liam yesterday, it was obvious you've still got issues. The way you reacted yesterday when you saw him.... I wanted to understand, but you kept on refusing to talk to me about it. I needed to know, especially after what you did to me. I'm sorry Daniel, but I had to know."

He folded his arms, his lips pressed into a thin white line. "What did she tell you?"

"Everything."

Their eyes locked. Lizzy's heart pounded. What would he do? It had definitely been a risk talking to Nessa without him knowing, and she wouldn't blame him if he got angry. She just hoped he wouldn't become violent.

"Everything?" His eyes narrowed and his breathing was heavy.

Lizzy nodded, her eyes round as marbles.

He thumped the table and Lizzy jumped, her hands flying to her chest.

"She had no right. And you... you, Lizzy. How dare you go behind my back."

"I'm sorry Daniel. But someone had to tell me. Don't you agree it's better to have everything out in the open?" She grabbed his arm again and pleaded with her eyes.

Time stood still. Lizzy held her breath.

Daniel lowered his head a little and crossed his arms, his lips pinched.

"I don't know, Lizzy." He shook his head then looked out the window.

Lizzy prayed silently.

He finally turned back but avoided her gaze. His body had sagged. "I didn't want you to know all the terrible things I did. But then the way I treated you yesterday, maybe nothing's changed." He lifted his face slightly. His eyes had lost their spark. "I can't do this, Lizzy. You shouldn't have married me, your father was right. I'm no good for you."

"No, Daniel." Lizzy gripped his arm. "We can do this together. Now I know, I can help. And we can ask God to help. I'm not letting you go that easily."

Tears welled in his eyes and he wiped them away with his hand. "I don't deserve you, Lizzy."

CHAPTER 12

The next few weeks passed quietly. Lizzy and Daniel spent their free time talking and sharing more of themselves with each other. They went for long walks along the beach, where the gale, whipping off the North Sea, invigorated them and breathed life into their marriage. They huddled in cozy nooks of quaint old pubs they discovered in nearby villages, and they went to church.

Lizzy was frustrated, though. She prayed daily that Daniel would find God. Really find God. He said the right words, and did the right things. They even prayed together sometimes, but there was no depth to his prayers, and she sensed he still didn't really know God. Not the living God she knew and had experienced first hand. She tried to talk to him about it, but he always skirted around the main issue. She never once got the feeling he'd ever cried out to God or wept for forgiveness. Maybe he'd done it in private, but she didn't think so. She continued to pray for him.

One day as they were out walking, she suggested they take a holiday. Her heart lifted when Daniel agreed, and so they made their plans.

"WHAT A LOVELY FEELING, to be heading away for three weeks," Lizzy said as Daniel pointed the Ford Escort southeast on the M1. "It's going to be so good to see Sal again." She glanced at Daniel and sighed wistfully. "Maybe not so good seeing my parents, but we should be able to cope with one night."

"Mmm. I don't want to think about it. I'm not looking forward to seeing your old man, and I guess he's not looking forward to seeing me either. It's surprising they asked us to stay after you turned the offer of the wedding down."

"I think Mother talked him around. I feel really sorry for them both, especially Father. He's so caught up with what people think and putting on a show to all their friends and neighbours, he can't see there's more to life. I'm not sure how I managed to escape from it, but I'm glad I did." She leaned back in her seat and looked out the window.

"They wanted me to marry this guy called Terence Allsopp. His family are just as bad, maybe even worse. I couldn't imagine being married to him and living like they all do in their big fancy manor homes." She turned her head and looked at Daniel. "You know, I think I'd be happy living in a tent in the middle of a desert as long as we loved each other enough."

Daniel laughed and threw his head back. "You never cease to amaze me, Lizzy. I can't see you living in a tent anywhere, let alone in a desert." He glanced at her. "Do you even know what a desert's like?"

She grinned, and her eyes lit up. "Maybe not. I was just making a point." She paused for a moment, as she pictured her and Daniel trying to put up a tent in the middle of a sandstorm in a hot desert. "Maybe not in a desert, but you know what I mean. I don't want a huge house. I just want a house that's a home, with lots of children running around playing happily because they feel loved. That's really all I want."

"And just how many children are you planning on?" he asked playfully. "Do I have a say in this?"

She laughed and her eyes sparkled. "Oh, I don't know. Maybe a dozen?"

He chuckled and shot her a cheeky glance. "And we're not even Catholic!"

Lizzy settled back into her seat and relaxed as the miles slipped by. She tried not to think about the night ahead, and instead looked forward with anticipation to seeing Sal and to the cottage by the sea they'd booked for their holiday.

"HERE IT IS…" Lizzy said hours later as they reached the stone pillared entrance to Wiveliscombe Manor, the impressive manor house she used to call home. Nothing seemed to have changed. The gardens looked immaculate as ever. Not a single dead head on the roses that filled the circular garden beds, nor a stray weed in sight. Everything in its rightful place. Her chest tightened as images of their last visit flitted through her mind.

"Let's stop for a moment, Daniel." She reached out and grabbed his hand. "I'm not sure I'm ready for this. Are you?"

He shook his head. "Don't think I'll ever be."

"I wish we could just drive on, but we've got to do it." She turned her head and sighed heavily as she looked at the house. "I guess we'd better go."

Daniel put the car into gear, and they slowly made their way up the long gravel driveway towards the house.

HAVING PULLED up in front of the house, Lizzy climbed out and was stretching her arms when she saw her mother walking towards them.

"Elizabeth, dear, how good to see you." Gwyneth reached out her hands and studied her daughter carefully before pulling her close and hugging her. "And Daniel." She turned to look at him, and hesitated. Her smile grew warmer and she reached out her hands to him.

"Mrs Walton-Smythe. How are you?" He shook her hand gently.

Lizzy rubbed her arms and looked around. "Where's Father?"

"He's in his study. He's finishing some business, and then he'll be out."

"I hope he's going to behave," Lizzy said, rolling her eyes.

"He's trying his best to accept the situation, dear. Come on, let's go inside."

Daniel carried their bags and followed Lizzy and Gwyneth into the entry.

"I've put you in your old room, Elizabeth. I hope that's suitable."

"That will be fine, Mother. Is Jonathon at home?"

"Yes, he's home for the holidays and will be joining us for dinner. He said he's looking forward to catching up with you."

Lizzy turned and saw her father standing at the foot of the spiral staircase. Was he pleased to see her or not? *Why can't he just relax and be normal for once? Why does he always have to put on an act?*

"Father. Good to see you." *Okay, I have to play act as well, it seems.* She walked over and kissed his cheek.

"Elizabeth." *Why can't he smile?*

Roger turned his head to Daniel. Lizzy held her breath and prayed silently. He held out his hand.

"Daniel." Lizzy took note of the look that passed between them. It definitely lacked warmth, but at least they'd shook hands.

"I think I'd like to freshen up before dinner, if that's okay," Lizzy said, mainly to her mother. "It was a long drive."

"You must be tired, dear. But you're looking good." Gwyneth smiled, and stretched out her hands to Lizzy again. "It's lovely to see you. But run along, and I'll call you when dinner's ready."

Daniel closed the door behind them, and placed their bags on the floor. "Just as well it's only one night. What's wrong with the man?" He sat in the plush green armchair and rested his feet on the matching footstool.

"So this is your bedroom. It's almost as big as our apartment."

Lizzy glanced around at the furnishings and old fashioned wallpaper, and the image of herself as a young girl seated at her dresser brushing her hair flitted through her mind.

"I don't miss it, Daniel. It wasn't a happy home. Mother

tried, but it was always uncomfortable when Father was around." She'd opened her case and was pulling out some fresh clothes.

"We don't have to get dressed up for dinner, do we?"

"Probably best to put on a clean shirt. Don't worry about a jacket."

"Good. I wasn't going to."

"Don't start, Daniel. Please." She sighed, and walked over to the chair. She sat on his lap and wrapped her arms around him. "We've just to get through tonight. That's all." She leaned her head against his, and then stroked his hair. "We can do this. I know we can."

LIZZY HELD Daniel's hand as they entered the dining room a short while later. The table was laid beautifully. She would have been surprised if it was any different. Her mother directed them to their seats in front of the fireplace. Not that it was on. Jonathon sat opposite, beside his mother, and her father sat at the head of the table in his normal place.

"You've excelled yourself, Mother," Lizzy said as Gwyneth served up a roast dinner with all the trimmings.

"Thank you, dear. I'm a little out of practice, now that it's just your father and me."

"It smells wonderful, Mrs Walton-Smythe," Daniel added.

"Please call me Gwyneth, Daniel. Mrs Walton-Smythe sounds so formal. And I am your mother-in-law," she said as she placed several roast potatoes on his plate.

"Thank you, Gwyneth," he replied, smiling at her.

"So Daniel, how's married life?" Jonathon asked.

Daniel glanced at Lizzy and squeezed her hand before answering. "Your sister is an amazing woman, Jonathon. Married life is good."

Her father had said nothing apart from grace, which had sounded stilted and lacked any real thankfulness. Lizzy glanced at him. He held himself straight, and his jaw was clenched. *Oh God, please let this dinner go smoothly.* She had a feeling, though, that a miracle might be needed for her prayer to be answered.

Lizzy's whole body tensed when her father put down his napkin after wiping his mouth, and looked directly at Daniel. His superior manner sickened her to the core.

"What plans do you have, Daniel, for bettering yourself? Being a hospital orderly is hardly a job to aspire to."

Lizzy glared at him. *Why are you doing this, Father?* She waited for Daniel's reaction with dread in her stomach. She glanced at him. His eyes had narrowed, and his chest was heaving. Her heart went out to him. *Daniel, please don't. Please don't react.*

"I happen to enjoy my job, Roger. It might not be as financially rewarding as some, but it's what I do." His knuckles had whitened as his grip on his knife and fork tightened. "I resent your insinuation that it's not an acceptable job for your daughter's husband."

"I didn't say that. But I do wonder if you'll be able to support her and a baby when she stops work. She is my daughter, after all, and I have a right to be concerned. Do you not agree?"

"Lizzy's my responsibility now, Roger. You have no need to worry yourself."

Lizzy smiled inwardly. *Go Daniel! Not many are brave enough to take on Father! And you're controlled. Thank you God.*

The conversation continued, a little strained, until Jonathon asked Daniel how the mood was in the north.

"Thatcher's definitely not popular. Things are getting tough. Jobs are disappearing." He glanced at Lizzy. "Not as bad where we are, but you can feel it. I think there's trouble ahead."

"You'd be used to that, wouldn't you, Daniel? Coming from Belfast," Roger said, his voice full of contempt.

Daniel lowered his knife and fork and placed them neatly on his plate before looking Roger in the eye. "There's nothing wrong with standing up for what's right. It's the likes of you, all of you who lord it over everyone else, thinking you're better than them, that's the problem. The upper class disgusts me."

Roger's nostrils flared.

No! Please don't start!

"How dare you speak to me like that. Don't forget you're in my house!"

"I don't care where I am. I'll speak my mind. I'm not going to be put down by the likes of you." Daniel pulled himself up in his chair, the vein in his neck pulsating. "Who said you were better than anybody else? You're just an arrogant high brow aristocrat who doesn't have a clue."

Lizzy gasped as her father pointed his finger at Daniel.

"You're not welcome at this table. Remove yourself immediately."

"With pleasure." Daniel stood and pushed his chair back. "Are you coming, Lizzy?"

Lizzy's pulse raced. *Oh God, why did this have to happen?*

Daniel breathed heavily, and his eyes had darkened. What should she do?

"I'm sorry, Mother. I'm going to have to go." Lizzy stood and placed her napkin neatly beside her plate. As she left the room with Daniel, she struggled to keep her anger at bay. *Why couldn't he have just let it go?*

"WHY DID YOU DO THAT?" Lizzy asked Daniel back in their room. "Just one night! One dinner. That's all we had to get through. You should have just let it go." She stood inside the door with her hands on her hips.

"He goaded me, Lizzy. I didn't mean to have a go at him."

"Well, it's done now. Either you apologise or we'll have to leave." Her chest heaved and her eyes bulged as she glared at him.

Daniel held her glare and pursed his lips. "I'm not apologising, so I guess we're going."

Lizzy's heart fell as Daniel grabbed his bag and started throwing his clothes into it. She shook her head, and tears began to roll down her cheeks. Why couldn't they have got through just one night?

"Can't you find father and apologise? Please Daniel?"

He stopped packing, and looked at her. "You can stay if you want, but I'm going. Please yourself."

Tears streamed down Lizzy's face as she watched him open the door. "Wait Daniel. I'm coming."

AS DANIEL PUT the car into gear and spun the wheels on the

gravel, Lizzy struggled to fight back her tears. She glanced back and saw her mother standing under the portico with outstretched arms. Her father was nowhere to seen.

Lizzy fell back in the seat and threw her head against the head rest. How did this happen? Tears streamed down her face.

"Where's the closest pub?" Daniel demanded as he skidded to a halt in the gravel at the end of the driveway.

Lizzy shook her head and pulled herself up. "No Daniel. Don't go out drinking. Please."

"Don't tell me what I can and can't do. Just tell me which way to go." He sat with his arms draped over the steering wheel, peering both ways.

Lizzy breathed deeply. Her body shuddered as she tried to control herself and think logically. She didn't like the sound in his voice one little bit. Where was the Daniel she'd been planning their dozen children with just hours before?

"We could drive on to Sal's. It's not that far, and I'm sure she wouldn't mind."

"No Lizzy. I need a drink. Which way do I go? Just tell me."

Lizzy sighed and inhaled deeply. "There's a pub about two miles down the road on the right that has some rooms."

Daniel put the car into gear, and turning right, he drove until they reached the Red Lion Hotel where they took a room for the night. He was still angry. He'd hardly said anything since they'd walked out, and he had that rigid look on his face she'd learned to detest.

"I'm going down for a drink. And don't try to stop me." The look on his face made her wince. She knew it was no use saying anything.

"Wait. I'll come with you."

Daniel stopped in his tracks and turned around slowly. Lizzy inched back, feeling for the bed. What made her say that? Her heart thumped.

"Well, come on then." Daniel pursed his lips and grabbed her hand.

THE DOWNSTAIRS BAR was already noisy. Daniel led Lizzy into the lounge area and left her at a corner table while he went and got their drinks. He returned with three - a squash for her, and two pints for himself. This didn't bode well. She refrained from commenting. Any wrong word could tip him over the edge.

She still had half a glass left by the time he'd skulled both. Lizzy's heart fell when he came back with another three drinks.

"Don't." He said as their eyes met.

Lizzy's body tensed. This wasn't going to end well.

After the next round, Lizzy said she needed to go to bed.

"Come with me, Daniel? Please." She hated pleading with him.

He walked her to the bottom of the stairs, and then pulled her tight and kissed her aggressively. His beer breath and wet lips revolted her, but she responded, not wanting to aggravate him further.

His eyes were already glazed, and his words slurred.

"I'll be up soon. Be ready for me."

Lizzy pushed back her tears as he slapped her on the bottom. Once back in her room, she fell on the bed and sobbed.

THE NOISE DOWNSTAIRS kept her awake. Lizzy turned on the light and checked the time. It was past ten o'clock, so last drinks would have been called a while before. That wouldn't have stopped Daniel from stacking them up, though. She sat up in bed and stared at the smoke stained wall. How did it all go so wrong? It was always going to be hard, but they'd agreed not to let her parents get to them. Easier said than done. *This wasn't supposed to have happened.* And on the first day of their holiday. A tear rolled down her cheek and landed on the bedcovers.

She got out of bed and poured herself a glass of water from the jug on the dresser. *What am I doing here?* She leaned against the wall and closed her eyes, her hands resting on the baby growing inside her. She longed to feel it move, to know it was real.

The airless room was suffocating. Why wasn't Daniel here with her? Why couldn't they have helped each other deal with it? Wasn't that what marriage is about? Helping and supporting each other? Not running off and leaving the other partner in despair and turmoil, while you go out and drink yourself silly. Maybe she should have stayed downstairs with him. *Oh Daniel. Daniel...*

She laid back on the bed, and sobbed into the pillow. She wanted him to come back, even though he was drunk. It had to be better than being in this horrid room on her own.

HER HEART POUNDED when she heard the door squeak open

sometime later. His heavy step and the stench of alcohol pervading the room turned her stomach. How many more had he had? She clenched her hands to her chest and prayed silently he'd forgotten his parting words. She just wanted him to hold her. That was all.

But he hadn't forgotten. In fact, he was rougher than normal. Lizzy could only explain his behaviour by assuming he was taking the aggression he felt for her father out on her. That night, she rued the day she set eyes on Daniel O'Connor.

CHAPTER 13

The sun, peeking its tentacles under the door, woke her before she was ready. Lizzy opened her eyes, and remembered. She reached up and felt her face, then her neck, and then her chest. She closed her eyes as tears rolled onto the pillow.

When she came to again, Daniel wasn't there.

Lizzy dragged herself out of bed, and carefully cleaned herself. She put on fresh clothing and went looking for him.

He wasn't far away. Seated on the river's edge, his legs dangled down the grassy embankment. His head hanging low, his clothes dishevelled, he looked like the drunk that he was.

She contemplated walking away. Going back to her parents, and asking for help. But she could never do that. Her pride wouldn't let her. Besides, Daniel would come after her, she just knew it. He wouldn't let her go that easily. *But would she leave if she could?* Her emotions running rampant, she was torn between leaving and staying.

Lizzy looked out to the fields in the distance beyond and prayed.

Lord, I have no idea what to do. Tears rolled down her cheeks. *I know it's my fault. I made foolish decisions and didn't trust you. I know that now. I really do.*

She turned and looked at Daniel. *Oh God, what do I do? What do I feel for him? We were so happy. But now, I don't know. I don't know if I can get past this.* She hugged her unborn baby, and closed her eyes. *I can't go on like this, Lord. Please help me. Please.*

SHE WALKED SLOWLY to the edge of the river and sat beside him, saying nothing. She stared at the water, so clean and clear as it flowed across the pebbles and the sand below. *Just what Daniel needs.* Living water flowing through the innermost part of his being, washing him clean, making him new. *But he has to want it.*

She finally looked at him. "We can't go on like this, Daniel."

Moments passed. Her heart was heavy. He looked up and briefly caught her eye before turning his head away.

"You need help. You're going to destroy us otherwise." She wiped the tears from her eyes.

More moments passed.

"You're right, Lizzy. I'm a failure."

"No you're not, Daniel." She looked at him intently. "You're not a failure. You just need God in your life. He can help you. But you have to want Him deep down."

He shook his head and gave a half-hearted shrug.

"I don't know, Lizzy. I'm beyond help."

"No! No-one's beyond help, Daniel. Don't think like that!"

He turned and looked at her, his eyes dull and lifeless. "I know you don't think I mean it, but I'm sorry, Lizzy. I really am. I don't know what got into me."

She looked at him, and for the first time in their relationship she felt pity instead of love.

"Okay, Daniel. Just this time. But believe me when I say that if you ever treat me like that again, I will leave."

She held his gaze until he averted his eyes and looked away.

THE SHORT DRIVE to Sal's house in Exeter was quiet. Lizzy had little to say. Although she drove, her mind was elsewhere, and the familiar countryside passed by without her really seeing it. She occasionally winced when she moved in her seat and her body reminded her of Daniel's treatment the night before. The thought crossed her mind that she could report him. But would anyone believe her? Her word against his. And then, where would that leave her? Daniel would probably never forgive her, and it would only be worse. No, she wouldn't do that.

She'd have to tell Sal. She wouldn't be able to pretend that everything was okay with her. Sal would know. But how would Daniel feel about that? He never talked about his problems with anyone. She sighed in despair. *God, please help us.*

The flashing lights ahead brought her focus back to the present. A broken down car, that was all. She looked at Daniel. She'd need to wake him up. They were almost there. She paid more attention to her whereabouts. It was all so familiar. Was it wise to have come back here so soon? The place where her heart had been broken? Where so many memories were waiting to be relived. She'd have to be careful. If Daniel knew the extent of her heartbreak, who knew what he'd accuse her of? Especially since Mathew lived nearby. Had she suggested they come here because of him? Just to be near him? *No. Definitely not.* This was her home, where she belonged. She wanted to come because of Sal. No other reason.

Daniel stirred beside her as she slowed down for a red light. She turned her head and looked at him. Sleep had done him good. At least he now looked human. His day old growth was dark and stubbly, and he needed a hair cut. Once again she wondered what lay ahead of them. Would they ever be happy again? Would Daniel ever find God and true peace and forgiveness? And would her threat of leaving be enough to prevent him treating her like that again?

"SAL!" Lizzy squealed like a school girl as she fell into Sal's arms.

"Well, look at you with your little baby bump!" Sal exclaimed when they finally pulled apart.

Lizzy glanced down and rubbed her tummy before grinning at Sal. "I didn't think it was that obvious."

"It's not really, but you're so skinny, it does stick out a bit."

Lizzy's grin gave way to a broad smile. "It's so good to see you, Sal. Have I missed you or what!"

"I've missed you, too, Liz," Sal said as she peered around Lizzy and looked in the car. "Is Daniel alright?"

Lizzy's heart raced. *No, he's not alright, and neither am I. We're a mess.* But now wasn't the time to say anything. There'd be time for that later. Hopefully.

Lizzy glanced at him and was relieved to see him combing his hair. At least he was making an effort. "Yes, he's fine. He just fell asleep on the way here."

"You must have had a late night at your parent's place, then. Did it go okay?"

Lizzy sighed and lowered her eyes. "Not really. I'll tell you later."

Sal peered at her with a puzzled look. If only Lizzy could tell her everything right now. Get it off her chest. Get some perspective. But it was too fresh. Too raw. And besides, she couldn't tell her in front of Daniel.

Moments later, he joined them.

"Sal! Good to see you," he said as he hugged her.

"Good to see you too, Daniel. What's this then?" Sal asked as she stroked his day old beard.

He reached up and felt his face. "Forgot to shave this morning. I might keep it while we're on holiday. What do you think?"

Lizzy and Sal looked at each other and shook their heads and burst out laughing.

"Well I guess that sorts it then," he replied.

"Enough!" Sal said. "Let's grab your gear and head inside. Got the gang coming over tonight for a get together. Hope that's okay with you."

Lizzy's smile wavered and her heart fell. Did that mean Mathew would be there? One part of her longed to see him. The other part knew it would be asking for trouble. Big trouble.

"You look like you both need a rest," Sal said once they were inside her small semi-detached she shared with another teacher.

"I'm okay for now," Lizzy said, "but I might need a short nap before everyone comes tonight." *Dare I ask who's coming?*

"Let me make coffee, then. I guess you've had lunch?"

Lizzy nodded and winced as she took off her jacket. "Coffee would be great." She took a seat in the kitchen, and was relieved to see Daniel sit on the couch and flick on the television. *Maybe he'll fall asleep again, and then I can talk to Sal.*

"It's a pity you're not staying longer than a couple of nights, Lizzy. But I might be able to get down to the cottage for a day or so. Two nights just doesn't seem enough."

"I know. I wish we were staying longer, but Daniel wanted us to spend as much time as we could at the beach." In light of what had happened, Lizzy now wondered how wise that was. She picked up her mug of freshly brewed coffee and wrapped her hands around it. She inhaled deeply, allowing the sweet aroma to tickle her senses. She brought the mug to her lips, and savoured the warm creamy liquid as it slid down her throat. "This is wonderful, Sal. Thanks."

"Is everything okay, Lizzy? You don't look your normal, happy self."

Lizzy looked into her friend's eyes. *How much could Daniel hear?* She shook her head a little. Her gaze darted to him. His feet were up, and he'd finished his coffee. He seemed engrossed in the programme he was watching, and wasn't paying any attention to them. She leaned in closer to Sal and whispered, "Let's go outside."

She picked up her coffee and joined Sal outside in the

garden. Leaning back on the bench, she closed her eyes and soaked up the warmth of the sun.

"You're not okay, are you?"

Lizzy slowly opened her eyes and shook her head. Sal reached over and hugged her. Tears streamed down her face as her pent up emotion finally escaped.

"What's happened, Lizzy?"

Lizzy wiped her face and blew her nose with the tissue Sal handed her. "It's the drink, Sal. He can't handle it. It makes him do things he wouldn't normally do." Tears streamed down her face again. "Last night he and Father had an argument, and we ended up leaving." Her body shuddered. "We stayed at a hotel, and he got drunk." Lizzy closed her eyes and paused, inhaling deeply. "He was rough with me, Sal. I didn't do anything to upset him. I don't know why he did it." She sniffed and wiped her eyes.

"You poor thing." Sal hugged her again, and this time held her until her sobbing had eased. "He has no right to treat you like that. Especially in your condition."

Lizzy sniffed and fought back a fresh wave of tears. "I know." She closed her eyes for a moment. "We talked this morning. He needs help Sal, but mainly he needs God. He's so insecure, and he says he feels like a failure, even though he puts on a good front."

"Yes, but what he did to you, it's not right at all. I've got a good mind to confront him about it." Sal's nostrils flared and her eyes narrowed. "He could have seriously hurt you, Lizzy."

"I know." *Do I tell her about him doing time for assault?* Lizzy's mind raced. *Maybe not. Who knows what she'd do if she knew.* She breathed deeply and wrapped her arms around her stomach. *Oh God, how did I get myself into this mess? Why couldn't I have just married Mathew? It's not fair.* Tears threatened to start falling again, but she took control of herself. *No, I can't think like that. God, please forgive me.* "We've just got to pray for him, Sal. Only God can heal him and make him whole."

"Yes, I agree. He needs to talk to someone. Get some counselling."

"Maybe. But I don't know he's ready. He doesn't like talking to anyone about it, even me. But we can ask God to bring the right person into his life when he's ready. Until then, I'll just have to trust God to protect me and the baby. He's not like it all the time. And I told him I'd leave if he treated me like that again."

"Good on you, Liz, but shouldn't you consider leaving now? What if he does do it again? It might be too late then."

Lizzy shook her head and sniffed. "No, I'll give him one more chance. I'm not ready to leave. I know it sounds stupid, but I need to stay with him. I really believe God's going to work in his life."

Sal squeezed her hand. "As long as you know what you're doing." The look in Sal's eye made Lizzy shiver.

Did she really know what she was doing? Or was she making a big mistake?

A LITTLE LATER, when they were in their room together, Daniel grabbed Lizzy's arm and glowered at her. "What have you been telling her?"

"She guessed, Daniel. I didn't have to tell her." Lizzy looked up into Daniel's dark eyes and took a deep breath to calm her pounding heart. Daniel didn't move.

"Daniel, what's happened?"

He glared at her, but he was controlling himself. Finally he let go of her arm and slumped on the bed.

"Come here, Daniel." Lizzy's voice trembled. She stretched out her arms to him. "Something's troubling you. Please, Daniel. Come." This wasn't the Daniel she knew. This was a different person. A hardened, unhappy person. And he wasn't even drunk. *Lord, what's going on?*

Her heart raced as she slowly walked towards him. *God, please help me...* When she reached him, he looked up. The hardness had gone from his face, and the Daniel she knew and loved had returned. *But for how long?*

LATER, seated outside in Sal's garden, Daniel took her hand.

"I don't know what happens, Lizzy. It's like something snaps in my head and I become a different person. I don't mean to get like that. It just happens. I don't ever want to lose you."

She looked at him with a combination of pity, love and frustration all at once. "I know. But Daniel, it mainly happens when you've been drinking. That seems to be the trigger." She had to tread carefully.

He stared at the garden. "You're probably right. But I hadn't been drinking when we were at your parent's place."

"No, but you let Father stir you. And then you went out drinking. So maybe it's what causes you to drink in the first place that's the issue."

"Maybe I'm just a failure."

She sighed in frustration. "How many times have I told you before you're not a failure? You've just got a problem, Daniel. And you need to get help. Underneath you're a caring, loving person. You're funny, friendly and intelligent. You just can't drink, because then you become a monster."

"But I like a drink, Lizzy. How can a man not take a drink?"

"Because you can't stop at one, Daniel, and that's the problem." She paused for a moment and looked at Sal's garden while she gathered her thoughts. Should she talk to him about God? About how he could be freed from his inner demons? She couldn't keep putting it off, but was now the right time? *Lord?* Her heart raced as she turned her head and looked him in the eye.

"Daniel. I don't think drinking's the main issue. I think you're carrying guilt about everything that's happened, and whenever you get in a tricky situation, you drink to deal with it."

Daniel pulled back and opened his mouth to speak, but Lizzy continued. "Let me finish, please. I know you've said you blame God for taking Rachel and Ciara from you, but I truly believe that if you'll let Him, God can help you deal with it all. He can take away the guilt, and He can help you stay off the drink. He can make you into a new person on the inside if you'll let Him. He loves you Daniel, and so do I. But you've got to be open to Him, and want Him in your life. He won't force you."

Daniel straightened himself. "You know I'm not into all that God stuff, Lizzy. It might be alright for you, but he wouldn't be interested in me. And even if he was, I don't know I'd be interested in him. I'll sort my own problems out." He leaned closer and kissed her cheek as he squeezed her hand. "We'll be okay, Liz. I promise I'll try harder in future. I'm sorry."

All Lizzy could do was smile. Daniel's attempt to console her was comforting, but without God's intervention she was confident there was little chance they'd be okay. All she could do now was pray for the Holy Spirit to soften his heart and for another opportunity to share with him.

She leaned her head on his shoulder and closed her eyes, allowing the late afternoon sun to warm her body.

LIZZY SHOULD HAVE BEEN EXCITED to see all of her old university and church friends again, but she wasn't. They used to be so close, but now, what did they have in common? She'd already heard from Sal about their successful careers and marriages. As far as she knew, they were all happy. How could she maintain a facade in front of them, and pretend everything was wonderful when it wasn't? She didn't want to pretend, but she didn't want their sympathy, either. Could she ask Sal to call it off? Probably not. It was too late for that.

Out of all their friends, she was the only one who'd moved away, and they bombarded her with questions all evening. Answering the same questions over and over again was tiring, especially when she had to skirt around the issue most of the time to avoid lying.

"And how's married life?"

"Oh, it has its ups and downs."

"I bet it does!"

How many times had she heard that?

"When's the baby due?"

"What's it like living in the north?"

"Do they speak English up there?"

"Where did you meet *him*?"

"What does he do?"

"Are you going to keep working after you've had the baby?"

"What do your parents think of him?"

"Why didn't you invite us to your wedding?"

"Have you got any wedding photos?"

"Sal said you were married at a Register Office. Is that true?"

"Why?!"

"Why not!!!!"

A few of the husbands had come, but they had little in common with Daniel. He made an early exit. He said because it was mainly all girls and he felt out of it. 'Have time alone with your friends,' he'd said. But she knew it was really because his heart wasn't in it either. They had much more serious business on their minds.

At least Mathew hadn't come.

Lizzy flopped onto the couch after everyone had left, put her feet up, and closed her eyes.

"You look tired," Sal said, as she sat beside her.

"Yes, I am a bit." Lizzy pulled herself up and yawned. "Thanks for organising it, Sal. It was good to see everyone. Strange, though. Living up north is so different to down here. It's like a different world. I got the impression they thought I was crazy choosing to move up there."

"They don't know the reason why you moved, Lizzy. Some of them guessed, but most just think you wanted a change, which is partly true. I wouldn't worry about it. You've got more important things to worry about."

"Don't remind me." Lizzy rolled her eyes and hugged a cushion. "I don't even know if Daniel's here. He said he was going to bed, but for all I know he could've gone out." She sighed and glanced at their bedroom door. *God, let him be there, asleep.*

LIZZY TIPTOED into the bedroom and breathed a sigh of relief when she heard Daniel snoring. Even though she was exhausted, she spent a few minutes in prayer before falling asleep.

CHAPTER 14

*W*hen Lizzy awoke next morning, her mind was in turmoil. Normally she would have been ecstatic if Daniel wanted to come to church with her, but this morning she was half hoping he wouldn't. What if Mathew was preaching? How would Daniel react if he met him? More importantly, how would she react if she saw him? Maybe she shouldn't go.

Daniel stirred beside her and as she looked down at his tousled black hair, her heart warmed with love for him, despite everything. Maybe this would be the day Daniel would hear from God. She'd go, and prove to herself and anyone else who was interested that she was over Mathew Carter, and that she was in love with her handsome, gregarious Irishman.

As THEY TOOK their seats towards the back of the church, the familiar surroundings of the church stirred Lizzy's heart. It had been in this very building she'd come to the Lord, and the memories she held were precious. It felt like home, even though it was only a building. Not much had changed. The well used hymnals still graced the back of the dark timber pews, but were now accompanied by the newer praise and worship song books some of the older parishioners didn't like. The organ played quietly as people continued to take their seats. Lizzy looked around discreetly and saw a lot of familiar faces. Her heart suddenly fell as she realised there might be a repeat performance of the question and answer time she'd suffered through last night. Maybe they should sneak out during the last hymn.

They stood as the music from the organ rose and began to play the first hymn. As she sang, the words of Blessed Assurance warmed her heart, and she was truly grateful that Jesus was indeed hers. Beside her, Daniel sang the words too. At the last moment, he'd decided to come, and she stood proudly with him, holding his hand. She prayed that one day soon he'd also be able to claim this as his story.

Her pulse raced when Mathew walked to the pulpit. She hoped Daniel wouldn't notice. Her eyes took in every one of his features. He so looked the part. She breathed deeply in an attempt to control the emotions she didn't want to be feeling and knew were wrong. She prayed for forgiveness and asked for strength, and then focused her attention on the content of the sermon rather than the speaker.

Despite her previous decision to sneak out, she couldn't do it. Mathew stood at the exit, shaking everyone's hands as they left. Her heart pounded as she followed Sal towards him. Her hands shook, and were clammy. She'd have to introduce Daniel to him. But would she be able to speak? She felt like a bumbling, nervous school girl about to go on her first date, not a mature married woman carrying her first child. *Oh Lord, please help me. This was a stupid idea. We shouldn't have come.*

Then he was there, standing right in front of her. The dimple on his right cheek appeared as he smiled, causing palpitations in her heart.

"Lizzy!" He stretched out his hands. The hands she'd held so lovingly in the past. The hands she could now only shake. She looked into his eyes, and for a moment time stood still. How she longed to wrap her arms around him, but instead, she turned and introduced Daniel. Had Mathew sensed any hesitation? Did he see the turmoil she was in when he looked into her eyes? She hoped not.

She laughed too loudly, and her voice was too high as she tried to cover her nervousness with meaningless chatter. Her eyes lingered on his as they walked away, and her heart felt like it was being ripped out of her. She prayed Daniel wouldn't notice.

"I NEED TO GO THE BATHROOM," Lizzy said to both Sal and Daniel as they reached the outside grassed area. "I'll be right back."

Standing in front of the mirror, she saw how flushed her face looked. She turned the tap on and splashed cool water on it until she felt normal and had regained control of herself. There was no towel, so she rummaged in her bag and found a tissue. That would have to do. She patted her face dry, and wiped away the mascara that had run and was making her eyes look like Alice Cooper's. She brushed her hair and breathed deeply, thankful that nobody else had come in.

She straightened her skirt, and turned sideways. She could just see her baby bump if she stood on tiptoes. Had Mathew noticed it? *Stop it, Lizzy. You can't think about him like that anymore. It's wrong.*

Thankful it was a bright sunny day, she hid behind her sunglasses as she opened the door and stepped out.

"So, what have you got planned for us for the rest of the day?" Lizzy asked Sal a little too brightly when she returned a few seconds later. She grabbed hold of Daniel's arm and gave it a squeeze.

"How about we show Daniel the highlights of Exeter? Are you up to riding, Liz?"

Lizzy hesitated for just a moment. "Yes! It'll be fun to ride. What do you think, Daniel?"

"Fine by me." But he didn't sound fine.

"Great! There are two bikes at home, and we can borrow one from next door."

Lizzy took one last lingering look at Mathew before they walked to the car.

It was a lovely day for a ride around town. They visited the cathedral and the university, and rode past the flat Lizzy had lived in whilst she was a student. Although she found it difficult, she didn't allow her mind to dwell on any of the memories that included Mathew. Finally, they rode along some of the canal paths and ended up at an old pub sitting on the edge of the River Exe.

They chose to sit on the terrace overlooking the river, and were lucky to get a table. The late afternoon sun cast its golden glow over the weeping willow trees standing on the opposite bank, creating a peaceful setting. Keen rowers were taking advantage of the good weather, as were a number of families out for a leisurely Sunday afternoon stroll.

Lizzy pulled her chair closer to Daniel's and took his hand. She needed to make an effort to keep things right between them. He was, after all, like it or not, the man she'd married.

~

WHILE LIZZY and Sal chatted away, Daniel sat quietly, contemplating the looks that had passed between Lizzy and her ex beau that morning. She'd told him it was all over, but Lizzy's demeanour suggested otherwise. *A man could get really jealous if he wasn't careful.* The all familiar aroma of the ale house wafted around him, tempting him to order a real drink. But he'd promised Lizzy, so he fought the temptation.

He lit a cigarette, and fidgeted with the car keys as he studied his wife. She was too good for him, if he was honest with himself. Why she'd ever agreed to marry him was beyond his understanding. They came from different worlds, he and Lizzy. What could he offer her? A hospital orderly's wage was never going to be enough to keep her happy. And before long, she'd be stopping work to have their baby. How would they survive on his wage alone? *It would have been better if she'd stayed with that preacher.* He was obviously more her type than him. Educated. Well behaved. Probably never been drunk in his life. Maybe he didn't even drink.

He stubbed out his cigarette and stood up. "I'm getting a drink. Do you girls want another?"

~

LIZZY LOOKED at Daniel in alarm and grabbed his hand. "No Daniel. Please don't," she pleaded.

His eyes had that unsettled look she'd come to hate. Why hadn't she noticed he was on edge?

Her heart cringed when he glared at her and pulled his hand away. "I'm only having one. I'm not getting drunk. Do you want another drink or not?"

Lizzy glanced at Sal, and then shook her head. She had that sinking feeling in her chest, as if a heavy weight was pulling her down and she could do little to stop it. She closed her eyes momentarily and inhaled deeply in an attempt to still her racing heart.

Sal reached out and squeezed her hand. Lizzy looked into Sal's caring eyes and fought back the tears triggered by her friend's concern and understanding.

"Oh, Lizzy." Sal squeezed Lizzy's hand tighter. "I'm here for you. Just remember that."

Lizzy nodded and wiped her tears.

Sal withdrew her hand just before Daniel returned. Lizzy's heart was heavy, but she made sure she involved Daniel in their conversation.

Daniel was true to his word and only had one drink, although the number of cigarettes he smoked suggested he was still on edge and could easily have had more. They ordered a meal, and then rode back to Sal's place in the dark.

As they prepared for bed later that night, Lizzy watched every word for fear of saying something wrong, and jumped at every slightest movement Daniel made. She just wanted the tension between them to disappear, and tried several times to wrap her arms around him and tell him she loved him, but he pushed her away every time. The silence between them killed her.

Her pulse quickened when he turned and glared at her. His eyes had narrowed and the vein in his forehead bulged. She leaned back as far as she could as he spat into her face. "I saw the way you looked at him, Lizzy. Tell me, do you still love him?"

So he had noticed. A bolt of alarm ran through her body and for a moment she was unable to reply. Was he going to hurt her? Her heart rate increased even further and she tried to stop her hands from shaking. She shook her head. "No. No, I don't love him, Daniel. It's over." She inhaled deeply as she waited for his next move.

He leaned so close she could feel his breath on her face. "It had better be."

She inched back on the bed as far as she could. Her chest heaved. They stared at each other for what seemed minutes. Tension hung in the air between them. Should she scream out for Sal, or just sit it out and see what he'd do? Rooted to the spot and unable to speak, Lizzy held her breath and waited.

Finally she spoke. Her voice was quiet. "Daniel, it really is over." She gulped and reached out to him. "It was just a shock seeing him again this morning. But it really is over. You need to believe me." She inched closer to him. "It's you I love, Daniel. We've got stuff to sort out, but believe me, I love you, not him."

But was it the truth, or was she just saying it to placate him and diffuse the situation?

The clock in the living room chimed ten. Moments passed. Lizzy gulped. She stood and slowly walked to the end of the bed where Daniel had remained. His eyes had lost their dark intensity, and his body was less rigid. She wrapped her arms around him and pulled him tight. She ran her fingers through his dark curly hair and kissed his neck. She turned his head to face hers and kissed him slowly.

CHAPTER 15

The following morning Lizzy prayed a prayer of thanks when it seemed her peace offering of the night before had worked, and she smiled as Daniel sang in the shower. In some ways she wished they could stay with Sal for the rest of their holiday. How would it be in a cottage on their own, with no-one around to call for help if she needed it? No, she'd be okay. She'd make sure Daniel got all the attention he needed. And God was with her.

Her chest was tight as goodbyes were said a little while later. "Make sure you come and see us soon," she whispered into Sal's ear. She waved all the way down the street until Sal disappeared into the distance and could no longer be seen.

It wasn't a long drive to Blackpool Sands. The directions provided by the landlady were detailed, and although they made a number of turns along narrow country lanes, they didn't get lost once. When they reached the cottage that was to be their home for the next two weeks, they were rewarded with the most beautiful of views. Perched high on a hill overlooking the brilliant blue sea, the 16th century white-washed stone cottage stood like a sentinel guarding the beach below.

Lizzy climbed out of the car and stood, arms outstretched, breathing in the clean fresh air and taking in the amazing view. As she looked out on God's creation, her heart lifted. She turned around and smiled at Daniel.

INSIDE, Lizzy ran around like a small child checking out each room, opening and closing cupboards and investigating every nook and cranny of the quaint cottage.

"Come and look at this, Daniel! We can sit here to have our meals. Isn't it wonderful?" She hugged him as he came outside to see what she'd found. They sat for a few minutes in the summerhouse just outside the kitchen, breathing in the heady scent of the jasmine vine covering the trellis. Sitting there with Daniel, gazing out at the azure blue sea, Lizzy began to hope that maybe they'd be okay after all.

TIME PASSED ALL TOO QUICKLY. Leisurely breakfasts taken outside, walks along the beach below, drives around the coast-line checking out quaint villages and rocky headlands. Lunches in pubs where history was etched in each wall, and dinners either at home or out, each day held its own magic, almost as if they were on their honeymoon again, apart from an underlying feeling that Lizzy had that something was still not quite right between them.

Even when they were laughing and enjoying each other's company, she was aware that one wrong word could send Daniel off on a drinking binge. Although he hadn't had a drink since that last night with Sal, and hadn't been drunk since the night they'd stormed out of her parent's place, his restlessness was evident by the number of cigarettes he smoked and his inability to fully relax. She steeled herself constantly for another interrogation over her feelings for Mathew, and mentally prepared answers just in case.

One day as she was preparing breakfast, Lizzy felt a flutter in her stomach. She wasn't sure what it was at first. Such a strange sensation, but then she realised. She hugged her tummy and called out to Daniel. She guided his hand to where she'd felt the movement. She looked into his eyes, and warmed at the love she saw there for her and the baby. He didn't feel anything, but it didn't matter. She'd felt it. The baby had moved. It really was there. Their own child. Maybe this child would help Daniel face his problems. But then her heart dropped. He was probably anxious after what happened to baby Rachel. *If only he'd allow God to wash away his guilt and anger.*

Every morning as she sat outside having her quiet time, Lizzy hoped and prayed that one day Daniel would join her. How she longed to share this most important facet of her life with him. It was like they were walking two separate but parallel roads, and she wondered if those roads would eventually merge or separate. She pleaded with God for them to merge. She prayed that Daniel's heart would be softened and he'd be open to receiving God's love in his life. But he never wanted to talk about it. He dismissed it immediately whenever she even broached the topic, so she just prayed.

The morning before they were due to leave, her heart fluttered when Daniel joined her. Maybe today would be the day. She smiled as he sat beside her and lit a cigarette. The morning sun was warming and welcoming on her body, and the sea below glistened as it basked in the new day. She breathed in the fresh air and thanked God for His creation and for His presence in her life, and for Daniel joining her. She remained silent so as not to spoil the moment, but prayed silently that Daniel would also feel God's presence as he gazed upon His beautiful creation.

The peace was broken when Daniel stubbed out his cigarette and asked her unexpectedly if she ever regretted marrying him. The question took her completely by surprise. Here she was, thinking he might want to talk about God, but instead, he threw this at her. How could she answer him honestly? Her body slumped, and her mind raced as she tried to work out how to respond.

"Well, do you?" His eyes were intense and unsettled her.

"Oh Daniel. Where did that come from?" She sighed and shook her head. "Surely you know how much I love you. Is it really necessary to ask that?"

"I think it is, Lizzy. You see, I don't really know why you married me or what you see in me, so it makes me wonder if you're still hankering after that preacher, even though you say you're not." He leaned back and crossed his arms, his eyes fixed on her.

Lizzy fidgeted with her hands and felt her wedding ring.

She wanted to look away to gather her thoughts, to be free for a second from Daniel's intense gaze, but instead, she held it. "Okay. If you want an honest answer, there have been a few times I've regretted marrying you. The times you were drunk and mistreated me. But they were just immediate responses to your actions, not necessarily to you as a person. Maybe we married a little too hastily, but I do love you, Daniel, and I don't regret being married to you. Do you ever regret marrying me?" She raised her eyebrows and tilted her head. Two could play at this game.

Lizzy smirked as Daniel struggled to answer. "See, not so easy, is it?"

He narrowed his eyes. "You have no idea what's going on inside me. You think you know what makes me tick, but you don't. You want to shove this God nonsense down my throat, thinking it'll make everything better. What a load of rubbish. There's no way he could change anything, if he exists at all." He sat up and lit another cigarette. "I regret a lot of things, Lizzy, but marrying you isn't one of them. I regret I'm not good enough for you. I think you'd rather have married that preacher, but because he didn't want you, you just married the first man that came along to try to get back at him. And that just happened to be me. But I guess you'll never admit that. I worry one day when you realise what a no-hoper you married, you'll just pack up and leave." He leaned forward and held her gaze. "If ever you do that, Lizzy, I won't let you take the baby away from me."

Lizzy gasped and her hands flew to her chest. That thought had never occurred to her. How could Daniel expect her to leave the baby behind? But hopefully it wouldn't come to that.

She moved closer to him and took his hand.

"I'm not planning on leaving you, Daniel, unless you mistreat me again. We'll work through our issues together, but we need to be honest with each other. Talk to me if you're troubled, and we can work it out. I just want us to be a happy family. You, me and our baby." She glanced down and hugged her stomach. "Okay?"

He stared at her for a few moments. She wanted to know what he was thinking, and what really made him tick, but would he ever let her get that close?

"Okay Lizzy. I'll try. For the baby's sake. But I can't promise anything."

Lizzy exhaled slowly and squeezed his hand. Another bomb diffused.

DESPITE THEIR CONVERSATION THAT MORNING, Daniel was quiet and withdrawn for the rest of the day. Lizzy felt like she was walking on egg shells and wondered why. Why wouldn't he tell her what troubled him, especially after promising he'd try. She really didn't understand him, that was obvious.

After lunch, Daniel said he was taking a nap, so Lizzy took the opportunity for a walk on her own. She picked up her Bible and headed along the top of the headland. Reaching a seat that some thoughtful person had placed there years before, she pulled her scarf tighter while she breathed in the salty sea air.

Her thoughts turned to God. How she needed Him right now. Although she'd assured Daniel she didn't regret marrying him, seeing Mathew again had unsettled her, and if she was truly honest, she had to admit that Daniel was right. She would rather have married Mathew.

The truth of that statement filled her with guilt. She lowered her head, closed her eyes and cried out to God. *"Oh Lord, I'm so sorry. I'm sorry for being so impatient and not trusting you to lead me, and for taking matters into my own hands. It wasn't fair of me to marry Daniel when I still loved Mathew. Please forgive me."* Tears rolled down her cheeks. How could she ever make it up to him?

She stared out to sea, not really seeing anything, but in her heart, she heard the still, quiet voice of God.

'My dear child, your sins were forgiven at the cross. I hear your cries of repentance, and I know you mean them. My loving arms are wrapped around you. Draw on my strength, Elizabeth, not your own. True love is an action not a feeling. Go back and choose to love your husband. He needs you. But know that you can't change him. Love him as he is. Don't dwell on the past, Elizabeth, but learn from it. Whatever happens, don't forget that I'm with you.'

Tears fell from her eyes as the assurance that the God of creation loved her flowed through her body. All her wrong decisions were forgiven, and her slate was clean. And God had his arms wrapped around her.

She remained for some time, lost in the peace and love that filled her heart and soul, and prayed for Daniel and their baby.

CHAPTER 16

The next day as she packed their bags, Lizzy's heart was heavy, despite her experience with God the previous afternoon, and her earlier misgivings about being in the cottage on their own. If only they could stay here, cocooned in this lovely cottage, away from the real world with all its troubles and temptations. But no, the time had come to leave, and she just had to trust God to be with them.

The street lights flickered on as they turned into their street. The sun had set behind gloomy grey clouds, and Lizzy sighed as Daniel parked the car in front of the apartment block. More graffiti had appeared while they'd been away, and a gang of unkempt youths in torn jeans and flannelette shirts sat on the brick wall smoking cigarettes.

"It'd be great to live in our own little house," Lizzy said as they carried their bags towards the entrance. "What do you think, Daniel?"

He held the door open for her and glanced at the youths. "It'd be great, but I don't know we can afford it."

"Yes we can. We've got money saved up. Come on Daniel, can we please take a look?" Her eyes pleaded with him.

He looked at her and sighed. "Maybe."

Lizzy's heart lifted, and as she climbed the stairs, she pictured a beautiful terraced house, with a garden filled with sweet smelling forget-me-nots and daisies, and a swing where she could sit with their baby in the afternoon sun. It'd be wonderful. They'd have an upstairs and a downstairs, and they'd have space! Nowhere near as much space as she'd had when she was growing up, but that was decadent, almost obscene. How much space do three people really need? A terraced house would do just fine.

Daniel bent down and picked up the pile of mail that had built up while they'd been away. He ripped open one of the envelopes and the colour drained from his face.

"What's wrong, Daniel? What's happened?" Lizzy looked at him with concern.

He hesitated before answering. "I have to meet with the supervisor tomorrow at ten am."

"What on earth for?"

Daniel glanced at Lizzy before looking back at the letter. "It doesn't say."

"Maybe it's just to catch up on something that happened while we were away." Lizzy leaned closer to take a look. "What else could it be?"

Daniel shrugged half-heartedly.

"I don't know."

THE FOLLOWING MORNING, Lizzy leaned over and kissed Daniel tenderly on his cheek before climbing out of the car.

"I hope your meeting goes well." She smiled at him and gazed into his eyes. Their holiday had done them good.

She watched him drive off, wondering why he spun the wheels, and then surveyed the cold, uninviting walls of the brick building in front of her. *Only seven more weeks of school to go.*

Aware of the children's eyes on her as she walked along the corridor to her classroom, she knew the time had come to tell them. She'd definitely miss the children, but to not have any preparation or marking… she couldn't wait.

She looked down fondly at the little blond haired girl tugging on her arm.

"Miss, are you having a baby?"

Lizzy grinned and ruffled her hair. Yes, she definitely would miss the children, especially this one. "Yes Hayley. I'm having a baby." Hayley giggled, and ran off to tell her friends.

Lizzy laughed to herself as she opened the door.

～

DANIEL'S FACE dropped when Lizzy left the car. He watched her walk into the school yard and wondered how to break the news to her that he was out of a job. Because that's what he fully expected to hear when he attended the meeting. Her words of the previous evening rang in his ear. How could he tell her there'd be no house? She'd be devastated. And she'd be furious when she found out why.

He thumped the steering wheel and started the car. He put

his foot down, spinning the wheels as he entered the traffic. Who had it been? Who reported him? *It must have been that cow of a woman at reception.* He thumped the wheel again and cursed her.

Sitting in the car park with his head on the steering wheel, his chest was tight and his breathing laboured. The meeting wasn't until ten am. Two hours away. Two whole hours. He sighed, leaned over the back and picked up his lunch bag. Not that he'd need it. He opened the door, climbed out, and went to work.

"Morning, Danny. Have a good break?" *Why did they have to be so happy and chatty?* He held up his hand and waved as he walked past the reception area.

"It was grand, thanks. Good to be back." His trade mark whistle was missing.

And there she was, walking right towards him. He glowered at her as their paths crossed. His eyes bore into hers, and he had a good mind to pull her aside and have it out, but thought better of it at the last moment.

He reached his locker and took out his key. Looking both ways, he held his breath and opened it. It was still there. He gulped, glanced over his shoulder, and reached in. Time stood still when he heard heavy footsteps stop behind him.

"What have you got there, O'Connor?"

Daniel slowly put the bottle down and turned around. His supervisor stood with his arms crossed and a smirk on his face.

Daniel's muscles tightened. Highly skilled at covering

things up, he had no idea how to talk his way out of this. He'd been caught red handed.

"Move." The supervisor stepped forward and reached for the bottle. "Follow me."

He led Daniel to his office, where the Head of HR was already seated at a solid timber desk surrounded by dark panelled walls covered in diplomas and certificates, obviously designed to impress and intimidate. Just like the Headmaster's office at St Pat's. Daniel could see no positive outcome from this meeting.

"Well, Mr O'Connor, take a seat." His voice was steady, clear and decisive. He locked eyes with Daniel for a moment before continuing. "You can't say you haven't been warned."

Daniel knew there was no way out. Yes, he'd been warned. No alcohol was to be in his possession at any time, and that included his locker. He'd been caught three times already. Twice drinking on the job, and once being under the influence at work. This was the fourth time.

"I was removing it from the premises, Sir." Memories of being hauled in front of the Headmaster on numerous occasions flitted through his mind. How often had he succeeded in avoiding punishment back then? Rarely, although he'd always tried hard to talk his way out of it. What were his chances now?

"Very commendable, O'Connor, but too late. Your employment is terminated. Take your belongings, and don't come back."

Daniel's gaze darted from one to the other. "But Sir, my wife's due to give birth shortly. We won't survive if I'm not working." He leaned forward and spoke quietly. "Could I please have another chance?" He looked from one to the other. "I'll get rid of the bottle, and you have my word I won't bring any more in." His eyes lit up and he clasped his hands together in his lap.

The Head of HR drew himself forward, his unsmiling determination showing clearly in his eyes. Daniel's shoulders slumped.

"I'm very sorry for your situation, Mr O'Connor, but it's your own making. Your employment here at this hospital is terminated immediately."

Daniel held his gaze for a moment before he stood and was accompanied to the exit by the supervisor.

He was tempted to ask if he could at least have his bottle.

HAD it only been twenty minutes since he'd climbed out of the car? And here he was again, but this time, knowing for sure he didn't have a job. Daniel thumped the steering wheel with his fist several times. *How do I tell her? She's going to kill me.*

He lit a cigarette and stared out the window. Time stood still. Cars came and went all around him, but he didn't hear or see them. Neither did he hear the wail of an ambulance approaching the hospital. His head spun and his thoughts were jumbled.

Somewhere through the fog that was his brain, a solution came to him. He wouldn't tell her. He'd spend his days looking for work, and only tell her once he'd found a job.

Daniel turned the key in the ignition, and drove towards town.

*a*s Daniel expected, Lizzy's first question when he picked her up that afternoon was about how the meeting had gone. He'd been thinking about his answer all day. He didn't wanted to lie, but there was no way around it.

"Oh, it was nothing really. Just a few changes to procedure, that's all. Nothing to be worried about." He quickly glanced at her, avoiding her eyes.

"That's a relief," she said as she settled in the seat beside him. "What a day! I didn't get to sit for a minute. My feet are killing me. I have to say, I'm looking forward to finishing. I think I'll be counting the days."

Daniel focused on driving in the wet weather. How long could he keep the facade going? He figured he had two weeks. She'd find out anyway when his pay didn't come in.

"Sounds like you need a hot bath, Mrs O'Connor. I'll cook dinner tonight."

Lizzy's eyes widened. "Really? That would be wonderful, Daniel." She leaned back in the seat and smiled at him.

DAY AFTER DAY for the next two weeks, Daniel looked for work. As far as he knew, Lizzy never suspected anything. Worried that someone he knew would see him, he'd prepared answers that would dismiss their curiosity. He'd tried everywhere, including his local pub, but even they didn't have any vacancies. No jobs were to be had anywhere.

On Friday afternoon, he took himself for a walk along the river. It was driving him crazy. He couldn't keep it from Lizzy much longer. He could maybe get away with saying there'd been a problem with their pays - that would buy him a few days, but no more. He'd played it over and over in his mind how he'd tell her, but it always ended badly, regardless of which way he did it. He'd become jittery. Not having a drink for the last four weeks had been almost a record. He was proud of himself, but now, with so much time on his hands, he continually thought how good a drink would be. He could taste the bitterness of the liquid sliding effortlessly down his throat, and he longed for the immediate relief it would bring. *No, I can't think about it. Don't go there.* He walked on. *God, if you're there, you'd better help me.*

He found a rock on the water's edge and sat on it. The water flowed slowly, grey and uninviting, reflecting the colour of the sky. He picked up some pebbles and threw them in. *"You know, God. I don't think you're there at all. If you are, you've done nothing for me. Nothing."* He thought for a moment. *"Well, maybe you brought Lizzy into my life, but that's about all."* He threw more pebbles into the river and watched them sink out of sight. *"Stuff it. I'm going for a drink."*

He stood, and drove straight to his local.

~

WHEN DANIEL WASN'T THERE to pick her up by five pm, Lizzy knew something was wrong. She'd actually been surprised at how punctual he'd been since they'd returned from their holiday, but hadn't thought much more about it. She'd just been relieved he wasn't drinking, and that he was helping her out more at home.

The one main thing that still worried her, though, was his resistance to God. She continued to pray for him every day, but she was impatient. She longed for them to share a common journey, to pray together, to read the Bible together, and more importantly, to bring up their child together in a loving Christian home. Although he came to church with her, she knew his heart wasn't there even though his body was. He'd even agreed to attend a small group meeting with her during the week, but she got the feeling it was just to keep her happy, not because he wanted to learn about God.

But there was always hope, and so she continued to pray.

Sometimes she felt like shaking him. Why couldn't he just let go of all the things he kept bringing up as arguments? He still blamed God for allowing little baby Rachel to die, and for Ciara's death. He often referred to the fighting between the Catholics and the Protestants in Northern Ireland, and said in no uncertain words that if that's what religion's all about, he wasn't interested. It didn't matter how often she told him that

God wasn't interested in religion either. 'He's just interested in you, Daniel, and what you think of Him. Religion is just what man has made up.'

Daniel wouldn't budge. He blamed God for all the bad things that were happening in the world. 'If God's so powerful, why doesn't he stop it all?' he'd ask. It didn't matter how many times she tried to explain that whilst He could stop it all, if He did, it wouldn't fix the root cause which was sin, sin that could only be dealt with when individuals repented and accepted the forgiveness that could only be found in Jesus. He didn't want to wave a magic wand and force people against their will to serve Him like robots.

But Daniel couldn't get past all the negatives, and see the grace and mercy God was offering him though Jesus. He couldn't see the forgiveness and freedom that was his for the taking. All he could see were wars being fought over religion, people killing each other in God's name, people starving and dying. His heart had been hardened by years of conflict and hurt, and he was unwilling to open it, and it frustrated Lizzy to the core.

It also annoyed her that God didn't seem to be listening. How much longer did He expect her to wait?

So, where is he? She peered down the street, but couldn't see him in the line of traffic. A feeling of dread gathered in her stomach like a ball of thick heavy mud. She looked at her watch. *He should have been here half an hour ago. Where is he?*

She had to do something. She couldn't sit and wait patiently any longer. What if something had happened to him? Lizzy walked to the crossing and waited for the flow of traffic to stop, and then crossed and walked to the telephone box. She rummaged in her bag and found the number for the hospital. She placed the coins into the slot, and dialed the number.

"I'm sorry Mrs O'Connor, Daniel hasn't worked here for the past two weeks." *How could that be?* Lizzy's mouth fell open and she felt giddy. Unable to formulate a reasonable response, she thanked the receptionist, and then slumped backwards against the wall. Her grip on the receiver loosened, and it was left dangling like a thick hairy spider in front of her. She closed her eyes. The noise in her head deafened her.

She couldn't move. This confining dirty telephone box had all of a sudden become her haven. Her protection from the world outside. If she remained here, she wouldn't have to face the horrible realities that awaited her outside. Outside, where everything had changed in an instant. *How had this happened? Why hadn't he told her? Where was he?*

The fog in her brain slowly cleared, and she realised it must have been that meeting. *But why had he lied?*

She turned her head when she heard knocking on the door. How long had that been going on? She made out a middle aged man through the filthy glass door making pointed gestures. She pulled herself up and gathered her belongings, and took a deep breath before opening the door.

She kept her head low as she passed him. The only person she wanted to look in the eye right now was Daniel O'Connor. She uttered a few words of apology as she left her haven.

≈

DANIEL KNEW it was too late. From the very moment he'd entered the doors, the familiar aroma of fermenting beer and cigarette smoke calmed his mind. The four pints he'd downed in quick succession hardly touched his throat, and now he'd lost count. In the back of his mind, he knew he had to be somewhere. He stood to leave, but staggered and fell. Johnno helped him up and ordered another.

～

THE TAXI DRIVER dropped Lizzy outside their apartment block. She'd thought about looking for him, but had no idea where to start. And how degrading would that be? No, she'd go home and make herself dinner and wait for him to come home. And then have it out with him.

But he didn't come home that night or the next. By Sunday morning she was ready to go out and find him. She couldn't wait any longer.

She telephoned all the hospitals in the area. No Daniel O'Connor had been admitted in the past forty-eight hours. She telephoned the police. No accident involving a Daniel O'Connor had occurred. He was not in their custody, but she was told she could lodge a missing person's report. She thanked the constable politely and then slammed the phone down.

She took a shower, dressed herself in the maternity jeans and smock she'd recently bought, and left the apartment.

CHAPTER 18

*L*izzy didn't know Daniel's favourite pub. There were so many, how was she going to find him? Plus, she was on foot. Daniel had the car. Her blood boiled. How dare he do this to her! Not only had he lost his job, he'd lied to her and disappeared with their car. Not normally an angry person, this time she'd had enough. Enough of his pathetic promises, of his insipid excuses. What was it about men? First Mathew and his pathetic reasons for breaking up. And now Daniel, unable to keep a promise, and wanting to blame everyone apart from himself for his problems. His weakness of character appalled her. Why couldn't he stay off the drink and face his problems head on like most normal people? What was wrong with the man? How had he so easily forgotten their agreement to talk about their problems?

She needed to calm down and think rationally.

Standing on the pavement, she wondered which way to go. The light drizzle dampened her hair and clothes but didn't dampen her resolve. She would find him, even if it took all day. A decision had to be made. *Okay God, we're in this together. You need to help me.* She took a deep breath and turned left towards the river.

LIZZY FELT uncomfortable and conspicuous walking past the neglected semi-detached houses that lined the streets leading to the dock area. What had drawn her here she wasn't sure, but she'd trusted her instincts and believed this was where God had led her. It was the kind of area she imagined people went to if they wanted to hide, and she guessed that Daniel was indeed hiding.

The street looked dreary. The front gardens, if they could be called that, were overgrown with weeds that flourished in this damp climate. Gates hung off broken hinges and were left half open. Some of the places looked completely derelict, not fit for human inhabitation. She hoped Daniel wasn't inside any of them. The smell was different, too. Maybe it was the mixture of diesel and rotten fish drifting up from the trawlers docked nearby, but whatever it was, it was pungent and stung her nostrils. The drizzle had increased to a steady downpour, and although it was summer, she shivered in the biting wind that blew down the desolate street.

She pulled her coat closer, and increased her pace. She passed a Chippy that was already doing a fair trade, probably not surprising since it was close to midday. The smell of frying fish and chips reminded her she should eat, but not there. Definitely not there. Just past the Chippy, the first pub came into sight. It was as she expected. A run down establishment that had seen better days. She really didn't want to do this, but she had to.

Lizzy strode to the door and pushed on it, only to find it wouldn't budge. Stepping to the side, she peered through the windows. *Empty.* She looked at her watch and remembered. Opening time was twelve pm on Sundays. Only ten minutes to go. But what were the chances of Daniel coming here at twelve anyway? He could go to any number of similar establishments in this area. Or maybe he wouldn't be at any of them. But there was no way she'd give up before she'd even started.

Maybe she should get something from the Chippy after all. She turned around and walked the short distance. The looks she received as she entered made her feel she didn't belong. Was she really that much different? Lizzy looked around at the waiting customers and thought that maybe she was. She stopped herself immediately. Wasn't that the kind of attitude she despised in her father and that she'd vowed to never emulate? But she had to admit that sometimes she struggled to see people as God saw them. She smiled at the shopkeeper, and ordered a packet of hot chips.

She just wished her voice hadn't given her away. A young lad sitting backwards on a plastic chair jeered at her. "Listen to her - poshness in our presence..." She cringed as his mates joined in laughing at the lad's apparent wittiness.

Walking out the door with her bag of chips, she wished she could find a place she really belonged.

LIKE WORMS COMING out of woodwork, at twelve o'clock on the dot, men appeared from all directions and converged on

The Sailors Tavern. From her position outside the Chippy, Lizzy watched closely. What was the attraction? Didn't they have families? What made these men, who on the whole looked clean and neatly dressed, flock to this dismal, uninviting, run down building? She really didn't understand. She watched for several minutes. Her heart pounded inside her chest. She couldn't eat any more of the chips. The grease made her feel ill, or was she just nervous about seeing Daniel and what she'd do when she did?

But Daniel wasn't amongst them. Her shoulders sagged as the stream of men petered out within minutes of opening time. Had she really expected to find him so quickly? She breathed heavily, and threw the remainder of the chips into the bin, then strode down the street to the next pub.

From a distance, The Hairy Hog had a similar appearance to The Sailors Tavern, although as she got closer, it did seem to be in slightly better condition. The outside walls looked recently painted, and unlike The Sailors Tavern, the colourful annuals trailing over the sides of the window boxes gave the place a much cheerier feel. As she approached, the raucous laughter flowing out from the public bar stopped her in her tracks. What was she doing? What made her think she could go in there and look for Daniel?

Lizzy retreated to the safety of a small park opposite the pub. Maybe she could sit there and watch and wait without submitting herself to the humiliation she'd feel if she entered the public bar. Maybe Daniel wasn't there yet and she'd be able to catch him before he went in. The bench seat provided a good view of the main entrance. Her eyes darted left and right, checking out every tiny movement that caught her attention.

How long could she sit there? She rubbed her back and stretched. It was useless... she'd have to go in, she was just wasting her time otherwise. She pulled herself up and walked back across the road. Her heart pounded as she opened the door and walked in.

The air was heavy with cigarette smoke and the stench of beer. She squinted her eyes to get her bearings. Had she imagined it, or had the din slowly decreased? She became aware of eyes following her. She walked slowly past the row of bar stools where men perched, leaning on the bar with a pint of ale in one hand and a cigarette in the other. And then she saw him.

It was obvious he hadn't seen her. She stopped directly behind his stool and glared at the back of his head. A general hush descended upon the bar. Daniel stopped mid-sentence and turned around, only to look directly into the eyes of his wife.

CHAPTER 19

*L*izzy's eyes bore into Daniel's. There was no need for words... he knew he was in trouble.

"Lizzy! What are you doing here?" He jumped off his stool and grabbed her arm. He needed to get her out of there.

"Get your hands off me, Daniel." She jerked her arm out of his grip and glared at him. She leaned in closer and hissed at him, "What are *you* doing here, more to the point?"

"Alright, alright. Let's go." He skulled the rest of his drink and stubbed out his cigarette. He glanced around at his drinking companions, and rolled his eyes to their jeers. He walked with her past the row of men who slapped him on the back as he passed.

Outside, Lizzy breathed in the cool damp air and crossed her arms. "What do you think you're doing, Daniel?" Her eyes narrowed. "I know about your job. Why didn't you tell me?"

Daniel hung his head and shuffled his feet. "I didn't know how to tell you, Lizzy."

"Look at me, Daniel." She waited until he lifted his head and his eyes met hers. The eyes that had caught her attention not that long ago were now bloodshot and fidgety. "Two whole weeks! Two whole weeks you've known, and you didn't tell me!" She leaned in closer to his face and wagged her finger at him. "And then you just disappear." The harshness in her voice surprised her. She took a step back. Her heart raced, and she knew for the baby's sake, if not her own, she needed to calm down.

"We need to talk about this, Daniel. But not here. Where's the car?"

He hesitated and then looked around. "It's down one of these streets. Not sure which one."

"What do you mean? Not sure which one! This is our car, Daniel, and you've just gone and left it lying around somewhere? Unbelievable!"

"At least I didn't drive it, Lizzy. That would've been worse, wouldn't it?" She jumped back and almost slipped as he stepped forward aggressively towards her.

She ignored him. It looked like he'd been sleeping rough. His clothes were filthy and his body odour mixed with the stench of stale beer and cigarettes made her sick. His shirt hung over his pants, half tucked in and half out, and his two day old beard made him look like the drunk that he was. She couldn't believe he was her husband. He disgusted her.

"Let's go find it," she said angrily. She grabbed his arm to make sure he didn't disappear. She felt his resistance as he tried to pull away from her.

"I'm coming. You don't need to drag me."

THEY FOUND the car two streets away, parked outside a derelict semi-detached house. Although it wasn't the street she'd walked down earlier, it could have been. She was surprised the car was still there, and appeared to be undamaged. She didn't even ask him if he had the keys. She'd brought her own set, and walked straight to the driver's side. She gave him no opportunity to drive.

He slumped into the passenger seat, and was silent the whole way home. She was concerned about how they'd get into the apartment without being seen by any of their neighbours. In the end, she decided she didn't care. She walked in front of him up the flight of stairs, and opened the door to let him in.

"I think you'd better get straight to the shower. How long since you've eaten?"

He shrugged dejectedly. "Can't remember."

Lizzy shook her head and breathed deeply. She'd need every inch of patience she could muster not to lose her temper.

"I'll make something, though you don't deserve it."

"Thank you." He looked up. "And Lizzy, I'm sorry."

Lizzy pursed her lips and took another deep breath. She stared at him before turning and walking into the kitchen.

DANIEL ALLOWED the warm water to run over his body, its soothing effect slowly clearing the fog in his brain. As his mind cleared, the sudden realisation of what he'd done hit him hard, and he wondered how he was going to get out of it this time.

He turned the water off and climbed out of the shower. Looking at himself in the mirror, he saw the dark stubble on his chin and rubbed his hand over it. Maybe he should he keep it? No, Lizzy probably wouldn't like it, and he couldn't afford to make anything worse at the moment. He opened a drawer, pulled out his razor, and proceeded to shave it off.

He felt much better, but hesitated before opening the door and facing Lizzy. He hoped she'd calmed down a little. He stretched his neck and shoulders, and breathed deeply.

～

LIZZY WAS MAKING coffee when Daniel entered the kitchen. She glanced at him. He looked almost normal again. His eyes had lost their redness, and he'd shaved that horrible stubble off, thank goodness. He also smelt much better.

He came around behind her, and before she could do anything to stop him, his arms were around her, and he was kissing the nape of her neck. She was tempted to allow him to continue, but her resolve was strong, and she turned around and pushed him away.

"Daniel, not now. We need to talk. This is serious."

"Oh Lizzy. Come on. I'm sorry." She side-stepped when he tried to grab her again. She almost gave in when she saw the playful look on his face.

"No Daniel. Stop it. Sit down. We need to talk about what happened."

She put the plate of toasted sandwiches on the table and grabbed the mugs of coffee she'd made and sat down. She needed to eat, but she needed to talk to him more. She took a bite of her sandwich and washed it down with a mouthful of coffee. She used those few moments to settle herself. It was going to be more difficult than she thought it would be now he was home, clean and freshly dressed. It had been easy to say the words out loud when he wasn't sitting in front of her. When her anger was at its height and she could have almost killed him. She prayed for strength to carry her plan through.

She took another sip of coffee and placed her mug on the table and leaned back in her chair. "I know you lost your job, but I don't know why. I can guess, but I think you should tell me."

She sat, poker faced, as Daniel relayed to her about how he got caught with the bottle of spirits in his locker at work, and how he believed he'd been set up.

"They wouldn't have sacked you if that was the only time, Daniel. Have you been caught before?"

He nodded and lowered his head.

"Yes. I was never drunk, though. I just had a swig every now and then to keep me going. It didn't hurt anybody."

"Maybe not, but it's against the rules. And you would have known that." Lizzy shook her head and took a deep breath. "Daniel, we can't go on like this. I know you'll say you're sorry and you'll promise you won't drink again, but how many more times can you say that? You need to sort yourself out, and I don't think you can do it with me around, so I'm going away for a while."

She saw the look of shock in his eyes but continued. "During that time, you need to make a decision. I don't believe you can do that on your own, even if you want to. The only way you're going to be able to do it, if you decide you want to, is to get proper help." She paused and took a breath. Her hands shook and her heart pounded in her chest. He leaned back in his chair and crossed his arms. His eyes had narrowed and she felt his anger building. Not a good sign, but she had to continue now she'd started.

"You need to get help, either with AA or the Salvos at one of their Rehab places. I won't come back until you're sorted." She gulped. There, she'd done it. Her heart beat even faster as he rose from his seated position and towered over her, hand in the air.

"You'd better pack your bags then and get out of here before I throw you out. How dare you speak to me like that!"

She stared him down. "Daniel. Don't." Her voice was firm and determined.

He lowered his hand, glared at her, then turned around and stomped out.

LIZZY SLUMPED in her chair and sobbed. Her heart ached. What had she done? *Oh God ...* She grabbed a tissue and wiped her eyes. *Maybe I should have been easier on him.* She sniffed and then lifted her head. *No, I believe You led me to say that. I have to trust You to work in his life, Lord. Please go with him. Keep him safe, and bring him to yourself, I pray. And Lord, work in my life too. Help me to grow and trust You more.*

She recalled the verse from Romans she'd read recently, and claimed it as her own: *'And we know that in all things God works for the good of those who love him, who have been called according to his purpose.'*

Lord, I trust you to work this out for good, in whatever way you will. Amen.

∾

Lizzy and Daniel's story continues in....

"FACING THE SHADOWS"
READ THE FIRST CHAPTER AT THE END OF THIS BOOK

Note **From the Author**

Hi, it's Juliette here. I hope you've been touched by Lizzy and Daniel's story so far. Their story continues in **Book 2,**

"Facing the Shadows" which follows on the next page. I know you want to see what happens, but I'd really appreciate if you'd consider leaving a short review on the first book before you read on. Reviews help people decide whether to buy a book or not, so if you could you spare a moment or so to leave a review, that would be greatly appreciated! It doesn't need to be long - just a sentence or two about what you thought of the book would be fine. Here's the link to Book 1. Just scroll down down to where it says "Leave a Customer Review".

Lastly, I fully realise that some readers will have found Lizzy and Daniel's story disturbing. If you'd like to read more about how women handle being caught in an abusive relationship, and why they simply don't leave, check out my post on the issue here: http://julietteduncan.com/lizzy-and-daniel/

Blessings,

Juliette

PS. Don't forget to read the first chapter of *"Facing the Shadows"* at the end of this book.

Contemporary Christian Romance
The Shadows Series
Lingering Shadows
Facing the Shadows
Beyond the Shadows
Secrets and Sacrifice
A Highland Christmas (Nov 2017)

The True Love Series
Tender Love
Tested Love
Tormented Love
Triumphant Love
True Love at Christmas
Promises of Love

Precious Love Series
Forever Cherished
Forever Faithful (coming late 207)

Middle Grade Christian Fiction
The Madeleine Richards Series

FACING THE SHADOWS - BONUS CHAPTER

"THE SHADOWS SERIES BOOK 2"

CHAPTER 1

*L*izzy rapped her fingers on the table, telephone held tightly to her ear. *"Come on Sal, pick up."* She glanced at the door slammed by Daniel only minutes earlier as he stormed out. Would he come back? And if he did, *what would he do?* Her hands trembled. She had to leave immediately, just in case. But why wasn't Sal picking up?

She threw the telephone back into its cradle, pulled the curtain back, and peered out the window to the street below. At the sight of the Ford Escort fish-tailing down the street into the distance, the reality of what she'd just done hit her like a ton of bricks. A sick feeling flooded her body, and she let out a desperate gut wrenching wail as she fell into the nearby chair and burst into tears.

With her arms wrapped tightly around her stomach, and her body racked by uncontrollable sobs, Lizzy tried to reign in the jumbled thoughts writhing formlessly inside her head.

It hadn't gone to plan. Daniel shouldn't have taken the car, *and where was Sal?* She should have been home. *Now what am I to do?*

A fresh wave of tears assailed her. Sal's mother had taken ill. *How could I have forgotten that?*

She pulled herself slowly up and dried her tears. That left only one option. She'd have to go home, but the very idea filled her with dread.

SHE NEEDED TO GO, or else the temptation of staying might be too great. Standing up, Lizzy straightened her dishevelled clothing and surveyed the apartment with a heavy heart. She picked up the wedding photo sitting on the coffee table and gazed into Daniel's sparkling, mischievous eyes. He'd been so happy and carefree that day. She smiled at the cheeky grin on his face. Then her heart fell. What had happened to them? She hugged her unborn baby and forced back the fresh wave of tears that threatened to besiege her.

Returning the photo to the table, Lizzy sighed dejectedly and walked to the hall cupboard. Her bags were already packed. Deciding what to take had been difficult. Where would she be when the baby was born? By then, hopefully Daniel would have sorted his problems, but three and a half months wasn't a long time, and there was no guarantee. One thing for sure - she wouldn't come back until he had.

Without a car, it was going to be challenging. Lizzy glanced at the clock. If she hurried, there might be time to catch the afternoon train to London. And then... well, she'd think about what to do when she got there.

She picked up the telephone and called a taxi. There was no

way she could bring herself to call her parents just yet. Taking one last look at the apartment, Lizzy wondered if she'd ever be back. Before opening the door, she grabbed the photo and squeezed it into her case.

THE RAILWAY STATION was busier than Lizzy had expected. Taking a train was a new experience. Her family always had a car, and she even remembered when she was little, they also had a driver. These days, Father drove himself.

Maybe going by train would be better anyway. If only she didn't have this heavy suitcase. She thanked the taxi driver as he lifted it out and placed it onto the pavement for her, but then she looked at the stairs.

Inhaling deeply, Lizzy picked up her case, and joined the queue for tickets, her heart rate increasing the closer she got. Could she really do this? Could she really leave Daniel and return to her family home? *Yes.* She had to.

If there was any hope for her marriage, there was no option. Yes, it was a risk, but staying was riskier. Daniel had to sort himself out. She couldn't do it for him. If he loved her as much as he said he did, surely he'd take action and seek help. But would leaving him like she had be enough?

Lizzy moved forward and gulped. It was her turn. The lady behind the counter looked over the top of her glasses with a bored expression on her face as Lizzy hesitated.

"Single to London, thanks. 2nd class." Lizzy's voice wobbled. She handed over the money and took the ticket. When would her heart stop pounding?

Although she'd left most of her belongings behind, her

suitcase was still heavy, and the prospect of carrying it up all those stairs was daunting. But she had to do it. She grabbed it with her right hand, and held the rail with her left. *One step at a time.* She could do this. Where was Daniel when she needed him?

Totally focussed on reaching the top, Lizzy jumped as a hand touched her shoulder. *Daniel? No, it can't be.* She turned around and looked into the eyes of a brown haired young man wearing glasses a little too big for his face.

"Here, let me help you." He reached out and took the case from her hand, warding off her protests. He carried it effortlessly to the top and waited for Lizzy to join him. "What carriage are you in?"

Lizzy took out her ticket and inspected it before answering. "Number three. But I should be alright from here." She smiled at the softly spoken young man who seemed more than eager to help.

"No, no. Let me carry it for you. You shouldn't be carrying it in your condition."

In her condition! She allowed a small grin to show on her face.

"Thank you. That would be lovely." Lizzy babbled about inconsequential things all the way to her carriage. What would he think if she told him she was running away from her husband? It didn't matter. He was only carrying her suitcase.

He helped her onto the train and lifted the suitcase onto the luggage rail above the seats.

"Thank you so much." Lizzy gave the young man an appreciative smile. "There was no way I could have lifted that up there by myself."

"My pleasure. I'm just down the other end of the carriage. I'll come and help when we reach Doncaster."

"There's really no need…"

"It's fine. I don't mind." His sincerity warmed her heart. There really were some nice people in the world.

She smiled at him. "Thank you. That would be wonderful."

He left, and she settled herself into her window seat for the first short leg of her journey.

Alone at last, Lizzy leaned back and breathed in the strange smells. People were still entering, and she hoped no-one would take the seat beside her. The last thing she wanted or needed right now was to engage in idle chatter.

Lizzy's head hurt. Not quite as much as her heart, but a trillion thoughts were running around in her brain, fighting for attention. She took out a notebook and a pen, and started a list. So many things to do, phone calls to make. *Nessa.* She needed to tell her she'd left, and ask her to keep a lookout for Daniel. *The school.* She felt terrible about leaving her class and Kid's Club at such short notice. She'd have to tell the principal it was unlikely she'd be back. He wouldn't be happy about that. She sighed and glanced out the window.

She'd have to call the hospital. Her next checkup was in two weeks. Then she'd have to call her parents. Or maybe she could just turn up unannounced? Was that a coward's way out? Maybe. She'd think about that one. She'd need to pay the rent on the apartment. Daniel didn't have any money as far as she knew. It was either pay it or risk losing all her belongings. She'd have to be careful with her money. The last thing she wanted to do was ask her parents for any.

And where to stay in London? It'd be too late by the time

the train got in to go any further, and besides, a day and night in London on her own held some appeal. Maybe she could stay two nights. No-one knew where she was, after all.

Now that her brain had settled, Lizzy closed her eyes and fell asleep to the clickety clack of the train.

She woke with a start as a loud voice boomed through the speaker. *"Doncaster. Doncaster next station. Change here for Kings Cross London."* She pulled herself up and stretched. How she'd slept in that uncomfortable seat was beyond her.

The train slowed and she gazed out the window as it passed the outskirts of the town. The steeple of the centuries old cathedral was just visible in the distance, but was then blocked by a coal train with seemingly endless carriages.

Once the train had pulled to a stop, she stood and looked up at her suitcase. No, she'd better wait. It'd be stupid to try to get it herself. She smiled at the friendly young man making his way around the other passengers towards her.

"Thank you so much. It's very kind of you." The young man reached up and lifted the case down into the passageway.

"My pleasure. I'll help you onto the next train, but I'm getting off before London. Is someone meeting you at the other end?

Lizzy shook her head. "No, I'm afraid not. I'll manage somehow."

Lizzy followed the young man to the end of the carriage, where he helped her down the step and over the gap between the train and the platform. But how *would* she manage? Her heart began to race as she gazed at the platform that stretched into the distance. And this was only Doncaster.

"The train to London goes from the platform over there. No easy way, I'm sorry. Up the stairs and then back down."

"Why do they make it so hard?" Lizzy grimaced as she looked in the direction he was indicating.

Shrugging, he picked up his own bag before picking up hers, and started walking. "Who knows? I'm Scott, by the way."

"Lizzy. It's nice to meet you, Scott." She smiled warmly at the young man and then walked beside him all the way to the next platform.

The London train was already there and filling up with passengers. Scott helped her into her seat in the seventh carriage, and wished her well. As he walked away, Lizzy was sad she'd never see him again, but content to be left to her own thoughts.

∽

TO CONTINUE READING "FACING THE SHADOWS", get your copy here

WWW.JULIETTEDUNCAN.COM/FACING-THE-SHADOWS/

NOTE FROM THE AUTHOR

I hope you've been touched by Lizzy and Daniel's story so far. You can follow their challenging journey in **Books 2 and 3** of the series, **Facing the Shadows** and **Beyond the Shadows.**

To make sure you don't miss any future releases, why not join my mailing list? It's easy to join, and I promise I won't spam you! Just visit **www.julietteduncan.com/subscribe** to join, and as a thank you for signing up, you'll also receive a **free short story.**

Could I also ask a favor of you? Reviews help people decide whether to buy a book or not, so could you spare a moment and leave a short review? It doesn't need to be long - just a sentence or two about what you thought of the book would be great, and very much appreciated.

Lastly, I fully realise that some readers will have found Lizzy and Daniel's story disturbing. If you'd like to read more about how women handle being caught in an abusive relationship, and why they simply don't leave, check out my post on the issue here: http://julietteduncan.com/lizzy-and-daniel/

Best regards,

Juliette

The Shadows Series

www.julietteduncan.com/the-shadows-series/

"Facing the Shadows", Book Two in The Shadows Series finds Lizzy in turmoil. Her heart aches for Daniel, who has yet to conquer his demons. As his downward spiral continues, Lizzy struggles to maintain her resolve and forage ahead on her own. With so much working against her, the reality of having to return home to the manor only enhances her sorrows. Lizzy knows the only way to win back control over all that haunts her is to face that which she has avoided for far too long, even if that means unearthing the truth behind her breakup with the minister, Mathew Carter. In order to continue her quest to move forward, Lizzy will have to draw strength from God and his healing touch, but only if her heart is ready to accept all that entails. Two souls united by circumstance, divided by pain, must pull themselves from the depths of despair and embrace all that is waiting for them and welcome God's gracious intervention in their lives.

Praise for "Facing the Shadows"

"A fantastic Book dealing with two of life's most difficult problems alcoholism and abuse. It deals with the love and forgiveness that takes to overcome the problems that a marriage suffers due to these issues. The book is beautifully written. You feel as if you really know these characters and feel their hurts long with them." *JoAnn*

The True Love Series

After her long-term relationship falls apart, Tessa Scott is left questioning God's plan for her life, and she's feeling vulnerable and unsure of how to move forward.

Ben Williams is struggling to keep the pieces of his life together after his wife of fourteen years walks out on him and their teenage son. Tessa's housemate inadvertently sets up a meeting between the two of them, triggering a chain of events neither expected. Be prepared for a roller-coaster ride of emotions as Tessa, Ben and Jayden do life together and learn to trust God to meet their every need.

PRAISE FOR "THE TRUE LOVE SERIES"

"These books are so good you won't be able to stop reading them. The characters in the books are very special people who will feel like they are part of your family." Debbie J

The Precious Love Series Book 1 - Forever Cherished

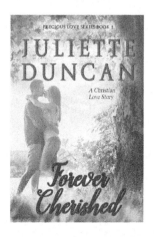

"Forever Cherished" is a stand-alone novel, but follows on from "The True Love Series" books. Now Tessa is living in the country, she wants to share her and Ben's blessings with others, but when a sad, lonely woman comes to stay, Tessa starts to think she's bitten off more than she can chew, and has to rely on her faith at every turn. Leah Maloney is carrying a truck-load of disappointments and has almost given up on life. Her older sister arranges for her to spend time at 'Misty Morn', but Leah is suspicious of her sister's motives.

Praise for "Forever Cherished"

"Another amazing story of God's love and the amazing ways he works in our lives." Ruth H

Hank and Sarah - A Love Story, *the Prequel to "The Madeleine Richards Series" is a FREE thank you gift for joining my mailing list. You'll also be the first to hear about my next books and get exclusive sneak previews. Get your free copy at* www.julietteduncan.com/subscribe

The Madeleine Richards Series Although the 3 book series is intended mainly for pre-teen/Middle Grade girls, it's been read and enjoyed by people of all ages.

ABOUT THE AUTHOR

Juliette Duncan is a Christian fiction author, passionate about writing stories that will touch her readers' hearts and make a difference in their lives. Although a trained school teacher, Juliette spent many years working alongside her husband in their own business, but is now relishing the opportunity to follow her passion for writing stories she herself would love to read. Based in Brisbane, Australia, Juliette and her husband have five adult children, seven grandchildren, and an elderly long haired dachshund.Apart from writing, Juliette loves exploring the great world we live in, and has travelled extensively, both within Australia and overseas. She also enjoys social dancing and eating out.

Connect with Juliette:

Email: juliette@julietteduncan.com

Website: www.julietteduncan.com

Facebook: www.facebook.com/JulietteDuncanAuthor

Twitter: https://twitter.com/Juliette_Duncan

Made in the USA
Coppell, TX
29 May 2021

56536573R20098